The Revelation

Leonard Bolanos

Contents

Prologue

The alarm on Nicholas' cell phone went off while he was fast sleeping with his face buried in his pillow. The alarm's loud hard-rock music startled him awake and made him jump for fear. The boy looked at the clock.

"Shit! Every day, staying up late screws with my life.

He quickly showered and then brushed his teeth. He dressed anyway he pleased, matching or not, and sped through the kitchen, stopping only for a glass of milk and two nibbles of a sandwich his mother had made. The boy gave her a kiss before rushing out of the kitchen, as was customary for him, in order to make it in time for the bus to take him to college.

Hey, hold on, sweetheart! I must speak with you. His mother said, but if he wanted to catch the next bus, he couldn't talk to her at that time. If he didn't forget, he would inquire about it with her at night.

Going to college and amidst the commotion created by everyone else, the lad anticipated a monotonous Monday with his routine classes. He didn't anticipate anything occurring. But Nicholas had no idea how his life would alter after that.

He began reading a book on celestial bodies and supernovae while paying no heed to the background noise. He had fairly romantic thoughts about the sky, seeing it as a place of limitless stories and possibilities. He had a fascination for stars, physics, and astronomy.

Like many others, he also daydreamed about becoming a well-known scientist and unlocking the mysteries of the cosmos. He would tremble when gazing up at the stars, as if he were being touched by all of those heavenly bodies or as if his body itself wanted to travel and communicate with the stars. It was as if the stars were calling for him. Undoubtedly, he enjoyed it. Because of this, he put a lot of effort into his studies and was able to attend the University of California in Los Angeles, the place where he resided.

But the lad also experienced a deep sense of emptiness in his heart as he saw his pals going with their fathers, a figure he had never known in his life. Since her husband had vanished before the boy was born, her mother has been juggling the two duties.

Nicholas exited the vehicle and entered the university. The campus was busy with people moving about to get to the classrooms, including professors and students. As soon as he entered the building, he ran into his friend Unquiet Sanches, a Mexican-American boy who was fluent in English because he had lived in the US for the majority of his life.

Hello, Nick. What's up, dude? We're beginning a new subject today; you know, the one we signed up for at the beginning of the term.

"Sure, yeah. It took so long to begin that I assumed it had been postponed. However, I'm excited to watch it. People claim that cosmology will help us understand the depths of the universe.

Sanches sneezed abruptly. He grabbed a few vitamins out of his bag and downed them with a glass of water.

"I have the flu once more."

"Friend, you need to look after yourself."

What do you think? You have never been ill before, not even the flu.

"I don't even recall getting sick. This seems weird to me.

The companion changed the subject as she began to watch the students moving through the area.

"Hermano, there are so many gorgeous women! You're going to find yourself a girlfriend this time.

"I really do. You are aware of how challenging it is for me to speak at the appropriate time.

I'll support you.

"I think nothing will alter if you're my teacher,"

Sanches took an inquisitive look at Nicholas' wrist as they both grinned.

Why never remove this bracelet, I ask?

"I got it from my mum. Before I was born, Mom claimed it belonged to someone she knew.

"It's awesome!"

It appeared to shine as Nicholas gave it a quick, repeated touch. The young man poked his companion to get his attention while gazing out the window in wonder.

"Look at that thing, okay? What a cool thing that is. He made a finger-pointing gesture. The question "Is it a meteor?"

Sanches immediately started looking outside.

However, I can't see anything.

I briefly believed I had seen a meteorite tearing through the sky.

"You seem to be getting excited for the class already. It seems even exaggerated, in my opinion.

The young man took another peek out the window, but nothing was there.

The topic of the day was the new subject. Due to a lack of qualified instructors, it had taken so long for this much-desired subject to be introduced. They were all eager to attend the lecture because our university will be one of the few in the US to offer Cosmology for study.

The pupils were eager to see the new teacher as soon as the first three fifty-minute lessons ended. Few students left the class, but many entered to participate in the new programme, filling it with onlookers.

The Physics Department's chief coordinator, Dr. Finken, intervened to address the ecstatic students: "Cosmology will now be made available to those who signed up for it at the beginning of the term. We apologise for the inconvenience, however after Mr. Franklin's resignation, we encountered some difficulties filling his position, which is why the lessons hadn't started earlier. Fortunately, after a thorough search, we were able to locate a highly trained individual to instruct you. He researches both the universe and certain important mysteries that are now known to humans. Please allow me to introduce Professor Glein, PhD in Cosmology, to the class.

The door was opened by Mr. Finken as he reached for it.

He said, "Dr. Glein, please come in."

The entire class was silent as they turned their attention away from the two men and towards the most stunning girl they had ever seen, leaving Professor Glein and Dr. Finken waiting for the applauses that would never come. The girl was a newbie who was standing at the door and whose breathtaking beauty drew everyone's attention.

The moment she entered, Nicholas was no longer in the classroom. Eyes wide open, all he could see was the girl's flawless feminine physique, which seemed as though it had been painted by a Renaissance master, with thick red shoulder-length hair, white porcelain complexion, blue eyes, and full lips.

"Holy cow, man! With a female that stunning next to him, lessons will be much more exciting, Sanches remarked, his mouth wide open.

I will say! She's stunning!"

Dr. Finken introduced the girl to the students after noticing the commotion she had created in the classroom.

The new student from the East Coast is this one. Let's introduce you to Zara.

Excited, the boys immediately got to their feet and began to cheer to warmly welcome the newcomer to the group.

Professor Glein, embarrassed, cleared his throat to calm the crowd and begin the class.

"At this time, Dr. Glein, I'll let you and the class work alone. I sincerely hope they enjoy Cosmology," said Dr. Finken.

Zara grinned in gratitude as she turned to face the students. When there was no more room in the classroom, she walked up to the seat right next to Nicholas and stared at him with the intent of unlocking the mysteries of his soul. When she approached him, he flushed.

I'm grateful; I can handle it now, Dr. Finken. Dr. Glein waved goodbye to Dr. Finken and added, "And I'm sure they will appreciate it a lot, understanding the Universe is really great indeed.

He then gave a brief introduction to himself before beginning to discuss his subject with the pupils.

"I have a degree in physics and a PhD in cosmology, as the honourable Dr. Finken stated. I'll start out by giving you a quick overview of what is known about space.

Nicholas noticed Zara looking at him while the teacher was talking.

She said, "Nice to meet you, Nicholas." So you're the person that excels in every topic in college, I take it?

"Hi-hi. My pleasure," the boy stammered, blushing, and unsure of where to gaze. However, how did you learn about my grades?

I assume everyone in this room is aware. Zara said, "You shouldn't concentrate on space to realise your dreams. The things we wish for may occasionally be there in front of us.

Nick was at a loss for words and was so preoccupied with his own timidity that he was unable to understand what Zara had said.

Wow, the most attractive student on campus is speaking to me! I can't believe that," he said, his mind racing.

Zara didn't stop looking at the student sitting next to her throughout the entire lecture, and every time their eyes met, he experienced something fresh and strange. His heart beat rapidly, producing beats he had never experienced before, and he pondered how a sweet, enigmatic girl like her could have managed to make him feel like such a fool.

This cannot be true. She isn't focusing on me. Just my imagination, really. She wouldn't ever develop feelings for a guy like me.

Someone poked him, breaking his train of thinking.

"Hombre, that girl doesn't look away from you. After class, go over there and talk to her," Sanches instructed him, grinning.

"Dude, I wouldn't dare. He returned with a mumble, "My legs are shaking.

Take a big breath, and go talk to her after class, Sanches instructed, placing his palm over his mouth to contain louder laughter. "Hombre, don't be a coward!"

The class came to a close when the bell sounded. As everyone left the classroom, Nicholas inhaled deeply to make himself bold enough to approach Zara and strike up a conversation. However, the poor guy failed to notice the step near the teacher's table and slipped, knocking over some classmates and creating a lot of noise. He was humiliated.

"The Moon Boy had to be it," Nick accidentally bumped into Adam while he was making fun of him.

Despite feeling embarrassed, Nicholas disregarded the remark, stood up, and walked to the corridor. Zara had already departed when he turned around to see. He had missed his chance.

After arriving home, the young man took off his shoes and relaxed before going to bed while thinking about Zara. He took some time to reflect on all that had transpired in the classroom and how upset he had been by the girl. Despite his inability to pinpoint what it was exactly, there was something about her that went beyond beauty and had touched his spirit. But Nicholas thought it was cool. He had the impression that he had already met her before. He made the decision to brush up on his college coursework after some downtime.

His younger sister Sophie rushed on him and gave him a hard hug as she entered his bedroom while still wearing her school uniform. She briefly fixed her gaze on the Cosmos book that was lying on the bed.

"Hello, bro. How did class go? Is everything okay?

"It was awesome! He said with a smile, "I met some new individuals, and something different came up too.

"Cool. I hope you enjoyed it. Please tell me everything afterwards. Mom is phoning to ask you to supper.

"What about you?" What about your schoolwork? On their way out of the bedroom, Nicholas questioned.

"The classes are really interesting. There are some obnoxious girls that occasionally pick on me, but I don't care. Louise, Katherine, Jim, and other nice males are also present. At break time, we all had a great time.

The two of them headed to the kitchen for dinner after updating one another on their lives.

"How are you doing, my son? I attempted to greet you earlier and say hello, but as it hit me... You were where? On the bus outside! Do you really need to be in such a rush all the time, Nicholas? Why not attempt to rise earlier? Living in such a hurry won't benefit you in any way. And lately, we haven't even talked much... Why not rise and shine earlier? In this manner, we would be able to fit in some morning discussion. Since Sophia's father abandoned us, I've felt incredibly lonely.

Nick's mother Lorena was that. She was a chatterbox once she got going on something.

"Mom, everything is OK. Not to worry. I swear I'll make an effort to go to bed and rise earlier. You're correct; we only have time to converse at night. In addition, whether or not Sophia is asleep, I also want to kiss her good morning. The problem is that I occasionally get into my books and lose track of time.

"My boy... Always a stargazer..."

Sophia's face was covered in a wide smile, some of her teeth having minor gaps in them. She was her mother's closest friend and was now eight years old. Sophia cherished her brother dearly.

"For this reason, he adores me! since I don't have any teeth! My tiny teeth are like dying stars, but I know new stars will soon appear to take their place. That's true, brother, isn't it? Sophia said, causing them to all start laughing.

Yes, my sweetie, you are my shining light. He gave her a hard hug as he wrapped her in his arms.

"Brother, you are loved."

When Lorena observed her kids having fun together, she grinned. She eventually said to Sophia, "Honey, you should now go up the stairs to do your homework."

I'm leaving right away, Mom.

Sophia hugged her mother and gave her brother a kiss. She then made her way upstairs to her bedroom.

The young man eventually went to his bedroom as well, still picturing the girl with the red hair who had appeared out of nowhere in his life.

Until his eyelids began to close, he continued to stare out the window as usual, thinking of Zara as they closed. The small youngster was completely unaware that a brand-new star, larger than all the rest, was throbbing across the limitless sky.

Chapter 1

Zara was now a further motivation for Nicholas to attend college. He tried to speak with her all week long. Despite the fact that they were seated next to one another and were regularly in each other's company, whenever the young man tried to strike up a conversation with her, he became silent. His head was jumbled with words, his palms began to sweat, his heartbeat quickened, his pupils grew enlarged, and he stared at her so intently that he unwittingly began to mimic her movements.

Both the girl and the boy placed their hands on the right side of their heads. Both of them rubbed their left eyes. She grinned, and there he was, awkwardly grinning back.

The poor gentleman mimicked the woman's left index finger spin of her red curls until he saw his hair was not as thick as hers. That was a tactic Nick kind of discovered unconsciously to get Zara's attention. However, due to his shyness, he wound up playing the fool and making her laugh each time she caught him doing something amusing.

However, just as he was about to ask her out or strike up a conversation, Nicholas became silent. Sanches made an effort to assist him after noticing his efforts. It was, however, improbable for him to remain amused by the circumstance.

"For God's sake, man! Work up the courage to approach that girl; otherwise, I'll do it on your behalf and ask her out.

I'm sorry, buddy! My mouth doesn't say anything.

Sanches mocked him with a smile.

"Hermano, if you want, I can talk to the chica on your behalf."

Simple, Sanches. When the time is right, I'll execute.

"I see. Good."

The young man thought about Zara most of the time as the days and nights went by. She occasionally muttered things in his ear, and he occasionally pondered about them and attempted to make sense of them, but most of the time he was unable to make out a single word.

"Nick, everything you currently see will change. She once said, "And I want you to view the true world through my eyes.

Every word she said seemed to be a mystery that needed to be solved, giving the girl who had been the sun of Nicholas' world ever since he first saw her an enigmatic air.

The young man then made the decision to ride his bike on the weekend. He did it almost daily since he wanted to connect with nature in order to unwind. He like the smell of the shrubs in the alleys he passed through and used to feel liberated when the breeze touched his face. Being alone and in touch with his planet gave him a sense of freedom that caused him to think about the stars. He could picture himself as a little dot travelling the world on his bicycle while being encircled by cosmic dark matter.

Without his knowledge, a small, round, silver object, resembling a drone, was seen hovering high in the sky and appeared to be keeping watch over him. Nothing about it reminded me of human technology.

He came across a wooden shack surrounded by trees one day as he was riding his bicycle. He disembarked out of curiosity to investigate the location that appeared deserted.

The cottage had two oak windows surrounding a little brown entrance, a damaged wooden gate, a porch with a low fence on the front, and a second storey with an ageing roof.

Despite his urge to enter, Nicholas became a little concerned when he saw that no one was inside and opted to continue riding his bike. He chose to pause on the way ahead at a little grassy field to take a short nap and daydream about the occasion when he would finally speak with Zara. On their first date, she would go out with him, and they would passionately kiss. When raindrops began to fall directly on his head from the sky, he was still seeing them dating and grinning at each other. He realised that night was approaching and was forced to return to reality just when his imagination was at its most vivid. He rode faster to get home as quickly as possible since he knew he had to pick up the pace or risk getting wet.

As the rain grew heavier, thunder and sporadic lightning strikes could be seen in the sky. Nicholas paused when he came across the abandoned shack that he had noticed earlier because he was unable to see anything further and because he had nowhere else to go.

Inside was pitch black. To check if the area was truly empty, the boy flicked on the torch on his mobile. He chose to remain on the porch because there was no one at all and his phone's battery was running low.

At that moment, he noticed someone going through the downpour. He could see a man moving in his direction. It was a person on a bicycle who appeared to be attempting to flee the storm as well. He could see that it was a lady as it drew nearer.

Nicholas recognised it even in the gloom of the approaching night, and his heart began to beat more quickly.

"That's not possible. She appeared here when I was thinking about her and dreaming of kissing her.

Zara came to a halt beneath the porch, rested her bike up against the wall, and pretended nothing out of the ordinary was going on while she gazed at him.

How about that storm? I'm relieved that we've reached safety," she remarked.

Nicholas inhaled deeply to try to control the range of feelings she had made him feel. Even more so now that the woman's wet clothing was clinging to her flawless form and her wet face was accentuating her gorgeous smile.

"Yeah! Fortunately for us, I don't believe there is any alternative shelter. The fact that you are here is such a coincidence. He managed to say, "I never believed you would enjoy biking as well.

Nick, that's a lovely coincidence. In addition to our shared love of the stars, we also share a passion for biking.

What do you think? In deserted areas like these, it is unusual to see an attractive girl like you hanging out by oneself. I consider it to be somewhat hazardous.

With the remark, Zara flushed.

"I do not perceive any threat at all. And the fact that I found you here is what really matters. Why is it that being by your side makes me feel safe?

We're secure in the cottage for the time being. Additionally, the rain will soon end. I appreciate your calling me Nick. Too many college students make fun of me.

I try not to be disturbed by it most of the time, but occasionally it irritates me.

"Yeah, you shouldn't give a damn what people think. Someone is always eager to criticise the way we conduct ourselves. Sometimes life changes so drastically in a short period of time that it is best to avoid wasting time on other people's viewpoints.

As their conversation continued, Zara began to describe the East Coast and its inhabitants. As he listened to her speak, the youngster dozed off and wondered what the flavour of her kiss might be. He was even more thrilled to be alone there with the girl who had such an impact on him.

"Nick? Hey, are you paying attention? She phoned him with a smile, "I feel like I'm talking to myself.

Nicholas turned to her and professed his shame, like any lad in love would. He would never consider embarrassing her.

The young man was fascinated as he saw Zara's mouth move seemingly slowly as she talked. The intense yearning to be near her had now taken over his body and soul; kissing her would feel like a supernova was being born on his own lips.

Nick would never be able to predict if the sun will shine for him again just as it was doing right then. He had been knocking on the door of an old hut when the rain, in all its force, had offered him such a priceless opportunity. All that mattered at this point was the appropriate word, the crucial action, and the precise amount of courage required to carry out his heart's desire. That peculiar circumstance might help him overcome his timidity a little.

Their eyes locked for a brief moment during which time appeared to stand still and nothing else could be discussed.

They could hear nothing but rainfall around them, and they both had a sense of unity and connection. Nick was breathing heavily and his heart was racing. He was no longer able to suppress his desire to Zara.

He approached her and put his palm to his face after becoming speechless. She groaned and went to sleep. Nicholas appeared to be under some sort of spell, his heart filled with joy. Despite the cold outside, he appeared to catch fire from the flames of yearning. He stroked Zara's lips and her hair, which had mesmerised him ever since he had first laid eyes on it. Then, caressing her tender skin as if with a touch of silk, he stroked his fingers down her face and neck.

The mood became even more nice as a sudden jasmine aroma was released; it was Zara's perfume. The young man had nothing else on his mind but her, and for the first time in his life, he let his emotions control him.

So, in order to avoid the possibility of losing his resolve, he drew up to her and gave in to the full lips of the girl who had touched his heart. He was seductively presented with her warm mouth in the form of a passionate kiss.

The surrounding trees filled the path with the fallen leaves that autumn had left behind as the rain had lessened a little. The surrounding fresh air was the greatest they had ever breathed.

Till the storm subsided, they kissed. She said, "It's getting late. Now I must leave. Tomorrow we have courses, so we'll definitely run into each other at college.

"Okay. What transpired between us today, Zara, I really loved. And I'll start counting down the seconds till I see you again.

She smiled delicately as she barely touched Nick's lips with her own before putting a finger to her mouth. She then proceeded down the winding route on her bike.

Lorena noticed something different during the young man's Sunday trip when he returned home with a gleam of joy in his eyes and such an unprompted smile.

Are you going to explain to us what has happened to you?

"I've never witnessed you so joyful!" said Sophia.

"While cycling, I met a great person. It was excellent!"

Knowing that Nicholas had experienced something new, the mother and daughter grinned.

"Mom, is it possible that Nicholas has at last found a girl-friend?"

"Girl, don't bother your brother."

The boy slept earlier that night while having dreams about their chance encounter at the hut.

Sundays became really enjoyable days once the new couple began spending every weekend together. While riding their bikes and sharing wonderful moments, they kissed and ca-ressed one other.

There was a sense of secretive cooperation in the class-room among the grins. The boy was disappointed that they didn't kiss or display any affection in front of others. However, when they were the only two of them and not in college, the world was theirs.

One of those rides had been unique one Sunday. Since they frequently passed the shack, one day they made the decision to look around to make sure no one had broken in and taken possession of the space they already regarded their own.

Zara approached Nick and extended her warm lips for a kiss, looking more stunning than ever with her face flushed from the journey. They were quickly accepted, and he kissed her.

Never before has he felt such intense affection for some-one. Everything about that woman was unique. She was the sweetest girl he had ever met. The young man pondered how he might determine whether she also loved him. Everything he desired after that first date was to remain with her forever. In addition to appreciating her in college and being moved by a true love, he had grown to care more about her as a result of the intensity of their shared experiences.

After their best date ever, Zara hopped on her bike and rode off.

"See you at college tomorrow, Nick. The time we spent together was wonderful.

"Me too. I'll see you at class.

A farewell smile from Zara.

Chapter 2

On the following day, Nicholas went over to his sister's bedroom and kissed her on the forehead while she was asleep. He got dressed on time and had breakfast with his mom, taking the chance to have some small talk with her.

"My time is getting tighter after classes started at the University. I would really like to be able to talk more to you and Sophia."

"I also wanted a lot and that subject about you not meeting your father."

"Please, I don't like to talk about it."

"That's why. I think your father's absence made you more insecure to face life. Everything will change from now on and someday you will need to manage on your own... You can ask for my support whenever you need it."

"I'll get over it. Let's change the subject. I met a girl. Her name is Zara and mom ... I think I'm really in love for the first time."

"Be careful, my son, don't get hurt. You are still very young."

"Fine. I go slowly and I don't even know if this is real. You know how insecure I am."

"Dedicate yourself to the course and go easy on dating. Anyway, I wish you the best of luck with her. Do I know her parents?"

"No. They're from the East Coast. Nobody knows her and I think she's a little mysterious."

They smiled at each other. Then he gave her a tight hug and left. Surprised by the change on her son's behavior, Lorena watched him and saw a pleasant smile never left his face. She was aware of what was happening to him and smiled, remembering the pleasures of being young and the happiness brought by the first love.

As soon as he got a seat on the bus, Nick wondered what it would feel like to see his beloved in the classroom after all that had happened on the previous day.

"I wonder if she feels something for me indeed, or if everything we had was just a fling. Will Zara respond to my love for her?" He sighed, picturing the features of her face, her cleverness, her sweet voice...

He got to college before the usual time and went straight to his classroom. Sanches arrived a few minutes later and, as soon as he saw his friend, he realized he was different from usual. He started to make questions in order to find out what was going on, but Nicholas said nothing, keeping himself distant most of the time.

He would rather not tell Sanches anything until the relationship was stable. His friend would no doubt ask for details he was not willing to talk about, or maybe he wouldn't even believe him and, on top of it, he would make fun of him all day long.

"You arrived earlier today, my friend. You always wait for me in the courtyard. What happened today?"

"Huh? Nothing at all. I'm just sitting here and thinking about life."

They talked until Dr. Glein came in. He greeted all students and started the morning class talking about the Theory of Relativity. All the students had their attention on the teacher's explanations, except for Nicholas, who stared at the vacant seat beside him. Where was Zara? Was she avoiding him?

Much to his relief, though, the girl arrived a short while later, late and looking distracted. She smiled to him and sat down beside the young man without saying a word. Also speechless, Nick smiled back at her.

At break time, the boy crossed the courtyard looking for Zara and stopped as soon as he found her.

She was having an orange juice alone at a table, while some students at the table next to hers watched her and tried to guess where she was from. "Typical youngsters who have nothing to do," Nicholas thought, for if they wanted to get to know more about her indeed, they should just ask her some questions, as he had done. It had taken him some time, sure, but he had done it.

"Do you know where the freshman is from?" Sam asked.

"They say she's from Florida, but no one knows for sure."

"I heard she has already lived in northern Europe, in Norway I think", George said.

"I can't understand why you guys think she's so special. She's just an ordinary girl and she's not half of what you think of her at all", added Beth who believed herself as the prettiest woman at college before the redhead arrived.

"As for me, I don't care where she's from. If Zara wanted to, I would go out with her right now," Sam answered.

"Hey, look at that! Isn't it Moon Boy? I wonder what he wants to talk to her about. Come on, we just can't miss it. It's going to be hilarious to see him getting dumped", Adam spoke smiling.

At that precise moment that Nicholas took a deep breath to overcome his shyness and approached. He kissed her on the lips and caressed her face. Then, he pulled a chair and took a seat. The boys, intrigued, kept their eyes on the couple.

"Could we speak for a while?" Nicholas said.

"Sure, sweetheart."

"I'd like to tell you I can't stop thinking about what has happened with us, and I need to talk to you about it. I have something very important to say."

"Nick, I also loved everything that happened between us. How about we meet after class today, at the same place? Is it ok for you?"

"Sure... I'll be there at the shack."

Zara put her hand on the back of his head and kissed him in a soft way.

He blushed and stood up, smiling.

"It can't be true. That's not true. Nicholas was kissed by the most beautiful girl on campus!" Adam commented.

"Maybe he's not as foolish as you guys think. Maybe you are the morons," said Crystal, a classmate who was at the table with them.

"I think there's something weird happening. The moron had never kissed anyone other than his mom and grandma for all his life, and in a sudden, the most beautiful girl ever, who leaves all boys gasping at her, comes up and Nicholas himself hooks up with her! Come on!" Adam spoke, annoyed.

Sanches got into the cafeteria and watched Nicholas and Zara kissing. Nick, who was just leaving, bumped into him.

"Hombre! You are going out with Zara, the hottest woman in college and didn't tell me about it? What kind of friend are you, hiding your secrets from me? A real hermano wouldn't do that. Don't you trust me?"

Sanches was very annoyed when he realized he had been the last one to know about the two of them, and Nicholas tried to apologize.

"I swear I was going to tell you, but everything happened so fast... I didn't think I'd hook up with her."

Sanches turned his back to Nick, who put a hand on his shoulder to talk, but the former got rid of his hand in a sign of his indignation.

"I'll try to talk to him later after he's cooled down," Nicholas thought.

Later, the boy rode his bike to the shack, and planned something to say while he waited for his love. On the porch, he felt like he was being watched, but he looked around and saw no one.

"I need to have the guts to tell her everything I feel. This time I won't lose my dream girl."

After a while, the woman arrived, went inside the shack and they kissed in a delicate way. He breathed and said:

"I love you, Zara. And I don't want to hide my feelings. It was great to caress you at college today, and I want to do it everywhere, every day, and no matter who is watching or not, get it?"

She knew Nicholas loved her and, somehow, she was getting involved with him too, but to her it was as if they had met long before.

Then, she realized that now was the perfect moment to tell him her secret, the real purpose that had brought her there, something that would change his way of seeing the world.

Just as the young man, Zara should have the guts to say the truth. And so, she did.

"Nicholas, I must tell you something. I'm not from here... I come from a place you've never heard of before."

"I was very curious to know where in the East Coast you're from. But it won't be easy to find a place I haven't heard about. I know USA's entire map by heart!"

Zara turned her back at Nick and gazed into a corner in the shack. For an instant, he wondered if he had said something that had hurt her. The girl went to the front door and the young man waited in fear that she was leaving. After a while, she turned back.

"In fact, I come from a place much further than a mere distant city away. I come from a planet called Life, in Andromeda Galaxy, thousands of light-years from here. As you may say: I'm an astronaut! And I'd like you to meet the crew I travel with. We are all scientists and we do research throughout the Universe. We decided to come to Earth because we need your help. Would you join us?" She asked, bluntly.

At first, Nicholas was shocked. Then he thought she was playing a cruel and foolish joke, telling him she wasn't from his planet. Since she remained speechless, he could barely believe it was true.

"What nonsense! She must be nuts. On the other hand, that would be the answer for everything. All that love couldn't be real anyway", Nicholas thought, devastated, unable to believe in what he had been told.

Confused, he could not understand why Zara was doing such a thing. Obviously, that wasn't true, but she seemed too smart and too self-assured to be nuts. Deep inside, he didn't believe she was crazy. He wondered if all of what was going on was a game. Maybe all she wanted was to joke with him. And Nicholas thought he was playing the fool.

"You mean we're not alone? You mean your ship could be here now, just above us?" The boy laughed and left the shack toward the road. The redhead followed him.

"Nick, wait!"

"Are they here?!" He started searching the sky for the ship. "Where is it? Is the truth out there for real? I just can't see anyone here!"

Zara screamed to make him stop pacing around.

"Close your eyes and give me your hand, Nick!"

The boy closed his eyes and smiled. She grabbed his hands and then his world collapsed...

Chapter 3

Nicholas opened his eyes and was shocked when he saw a world, he had thought possible nowhere but in Sci-Fi books and movies. He soon realized he was surrounded by extraordinary technology, composed by a vast number of tools which functions he could barely imagine. He was inside a big circular shaped lounge that seemed to be made of stainless steel and glass. He looked up and watched the silver ceiling with a blue light in the center just above his head. 3D holographic panels surrounded the lounge, showing lots of virtual graphics.

Although dazzled by so much that was going on, the boy realized he was inside a spaceship. The place presented excellent hygiene conditions, and many tiny white details could be seen on the command bridge. Nicholas touched the polished surface that covered a kind of control center of the equipment to check if all of that was real. Then, he took a deep breath and checked if there was a different smell around. He felt a scent of jasmine, recognized it, and widened his eyes searching the place for Zara, because he knew that was her fragrance. However, there was no one around. Silence was his sole company there.

Feeling cornered and confused, he took out his cell phone to try to call his mother or Sanches. But the device didn't work and he realized he was lonely.

Still feeling lost and afraid, he could only admire the ship's high technology. He recognized the Milky Way, that rotated in a slow motion in a holographic projection that came from a rounded source.

The projected image highlighted a blue sphere that spun around and floated on Orion's arm. Nick could recognize his home anywhere he saw it. That was Earth. "The most beautiful and perfect planet of the Universe", he thought while his eyes were fixed on the 3D projection. He also recognized the Andromeda Galaxy. Another globe was also highlighted in the hologram, as if it was being monitored. The boy realized there was something special about it and wanted to know its name.

"Which planet is that? How did I get here? Where's Zara? Am I dreaming?"

Many unanswered questions sprouted up in his mind.

Astonished, he kept admiring the high technology of the ship. He saw that one of the walls was made of something like glass, somewhat transparent, and allowed the crew to see what was going on outdoors. Everything there was quite intriguing. Nicholas got close enough to the glass to see planet Earth right below. Seeing it from above, he could watch its rounded surface and how tiny it seemed to be.

He saw how the blue oceans went around the brown and green parts spread all over the globe. Cities, countries, continents, and islands were in a non-stop circular movement, one of them covered by heavy clouds from which flashes of lightning came out, looking like mere sparks from a distance. He could linger there and watch that amazing show for hours.

"I've never thought I'd see such a fabulous thing in my life", the boy though, touched by it.

He turned his eyes to the walls that surrounded him. They were coated with some silver material that resembled a mirror, painted in a pale shade that reflected light all over the place. Nick couldn't identify what material they were made of. "I wonder if it's some kind of energy-saving technology."

The size of that lounge was something that intrigued him too. It seemed to measure something around 100 yards and it made him think about how big that spacecraft might be. He could not see any buttons or levers; as it seemed, everything was manipulated by holographic image. There was too much information and everything was too surrealistic even for a mind like his.

In a sudden, a door opened in the middle of the steel wall and a familiar girl showed up in a white uniform. Zara walked toward him, realized he was nervous and gave him a delicate smile.

"Nick, calm down. I know it's too much information for now, but I'm going to tell you everything I can."

The young man tried not to freak out, even though his body was trembling with the possibility that everything that was happening could be real. His eyes wandered adrift through the spaceship. He couldn't believe everything Zara had said was true. The woman stepped forward and touched his arm in support.

"Nick, are you well?"

"I admit I'm a little nervous. I still cannot understand what's happening..."

"Please, relax. I promise you'll learn more than you ever thought about the stars very soon. And I'm sure you'll like it."

She was silent for a moment, as if bracing herself to what she was about to say.

"We came to Earth on a special mission to find you. And we have a particular reason for that", Zara started. "I got into the university you go to because of this. It was easy to get there because it's not hard for us to access and manipulate Earth's systems of information. My plan was just to find you and convince you to help us, but when I got used to this body..." The woman said lifting her arms, "I shared the same sensations and desires you, humans, do, and it was impossible for me to avoid having feelings for you, Nick. That's why I gave myself to you without any hesitation, and that was wonderful! I know you have many questions about us, but we'll talk about it later, ok? And with no witnesses", she said under her breath. "For now, just relax, please".

"I'm sorry? You mean, you aren't the girl I met? The one with those perfect physical features, sweet and affectionate, who whispered nice words into my ears? Who are you for real? Why did you make me fall for you?" Nicholas said on the verge of insanity.

For a short while, the young man felt as if he was delirious. Aware of the situation, Zara hugged him trying to calm him down. At first, he tried to get away but, weakened and insecure as he was, he gave in and accepted the support from the girl he was in love with. Then he pushed her away with his hands as he tried to find answers to what was happening.

"Nick, please, calm down. I'm going to tell you everything, and you'll see it's for a good cause."

The boy couldn't understand very well what the redhead was saying, but he had no time to think about it because three men came in through a door, he hadn't noticed yet. And despite Zara's words to soothe him, he broke out in a cold sweat, his heart pounding.

"If she came to me in human shape, these guys may be doing the same", Nicholas thought, feeling nervous; his mind calculating the possibilities. "Will they suck onto my brain? Make experiment with me? Will they take me to space? It's a dream and I'm going to wake up! It has to be a dream! I trusted Zara, although now I realize I don't know her for sure. And what if she can't be trusted? What if she and these three strangers plan to cause me harm? Who are they in fact?"

There wasn't much time left for other thoughts. Soon, one of them stepped forward and, judging by his behavior, he seemed to be the leader.

"Greetings! My name is Sivoc, and I'm the Commander in charge of this ship. I believe Zara has already told you where we're all from."

Nicholas took a deep breath and widened his eyes, bracing himself for what could come next. There was no way out. To be able to know what that strange being had to say, he was all ears.

The commander looked like any ordinary terrestrial. Tall, with Asian features, light brown eyes, straight black hair, and a broad smile, he wore a blue uniform made of sparkling fabric, which brightened up when touched by light.

His serious facial expression showed certain concern when he looked at the other members of his crew. One of them sat down and started to manipulate the holographic images. The girl was standing very quiet, just watching the events unfold. Another man was standing around paying attention to the conversation.

"I'm... My name is Nicholas. I live in Los Angeles", Nick answered, stammering.

The Commandant smiled, trying to make him more comfortable.

"We already know enough about you, Nicholas, and it's a pleasure to meet you in person. Now, let me introduce you to the other members of the crew. At the control panel, we have Drako", he made a gesture toward the man beside him. "And that's Tibor, our chief of security. Zara, the member of the crew that you met before, is our physician and genetic engineer. There are also more people here in charge of all control systems of the spacecraft, but you will meet them as time goes by."

Nicholas looked at each of them while they were introduced to him. All of them had a human shape, as well as Zara and Sivoc. Drako had black skin, his hair was trimmed close to his scalp and he was very tall too. He greeted Nick from his position at the navigational command center and continued controlling everything with a slight movement of his fingers, which manipulated the holographic panels of the spaceship. Tibor was the tallest of them all, and had a very serious look on his face. His fair skin was filled with strong muscles. One of his eyes was red and he also had a robotic arm.

"We're all from Planet Life, which is approximately a three-million-year journey from your Earth. That is, in light-speed, of course." Sivoc said looking at the bracelet the young student had on his wrist.

Then the commander looked at Zara.

"Did you give the boy one of our bracelets?"

Everyone looked at the object.

"No. I thought it was an imitation like the props that exist on Earth."

Sivoc touched the bracelet and regarded it as if he were looking at a work of art.

"I's from our planet. How did you get it, Nicholas?"

"My mother gave it to me when I was very young. She said someone gave her a gift a long time ago."

"Very interesting. Then we will try to solve this mystery."

Everyone looked at each other curiously.

Nicholas watched his hosts with attention, and he wasn't sure what kind of question he would choose to start solving his inquiries. He had no idea of the things that would be later revealed to him and how they would make him much more amazed than he was with all that spatial vision he had had so far.

The young man went on watching the instruments that still made him amazed. It seemed like the navigator had total control of the equipment through telepathy.

"Drako, take us out of here right now", Sivoc ordered in a calm tone, but assertively. He turned to Nicholas and told him about the maneuver they were about to manage.

"Although space technology of the terrestrial governments is rather outdated compared to our standards, humans have special radars that can monitor us. Thus, it is of great importance that our personal contact here is short. That's why we must leave this place urgently. You should keep calm, though, because we don't want to cause you any harm."

"Sorry, but what do you mean? Where are you taking me?" The boy was terrified.

"Don't worry Nick. We are just trying to hide the ship from the terrestrial radars." Zara said trying to calm him down.

The spacecraft ascended rapidly. Nicholas moved toward the glass wall, and seeing himself in a sort of virtual nightmare, he saw planet Earth being left behind.

"I was abducted", he realized.

The vessel was at its highest speed now, and it went towards the moon. The earthling was in a jam; how could he run away from this?

Chapter 4

The boy had his eyes fixed on the Moon. The fear of distancing from planet Earth was gradually replaced by the wonder of seeing the stars he had studied and dreamed up close, the constellations, the beautiful and solitary immensity of the Universe. His eyes started to get watery when he thought of his family, which was getting further and further away from him as time went by. Perhaps if Sanches were there, he could also help with his peculiar optimism.

Zara stood next to him and grabbed his hand, showing him that everything that was happening was real. She knew how attached he was to his family.

"I'm here by your side, Nicholas. Please, don't worry. Even with so much for you to understand I can tell you I'll protect your life as if it were mine. About your family, soon you'll be with your mom and sister again."

He wanted to believe in the woman's words very much, but he couldn't, and no matter how good it was to be by her side, things were too strange and surreal by now. If everything she was saying was true, there was no way out. How could he manage to escape from the spaceship without a battle with its crew? Worst of all, how would he go back home? What was left for him to do now was to go ahead in that adventure and wait for a better chance to escape.

Aware of Nick's insecurity, the girl decided to take care of him affectionately. She knew he needed time to believe in everything that had been said. From now on, all information that would be given to him would change his opinion of reality as he knew it.

The boy would see the world from another perspective.

Zara hugged him affectionately while he watched the immensity of the Cosmos. Despite that surreal situation, he was attracted to that woman who made him fall in love for the first time in his life.

Within seconds, the Moon showed itself bigger and closer. It was bright, lit by the Sun, rays of light sparkling around it. It was such a wonderful vision.

If Nick already loved to watch Earth's natural satellite when it was full and from a distance, watching it so near was the epitome of beauty for him. On his right side, he could see the blue globe he called home, a giant home for billions of human beings. He felt like an astronaut, and he could have an idea of how euphoric the astronauts themselves must have been when they saw our planet and its satellite for the first time from such a privileged angle.

He saw its huge and grey craters as if in a big sandy desert with no living soul on its surface. He saw its dark plains full of depressions formed by craters which have been made by the comets and asteroids' hits for millions of years. He looked further away and saw some parts formed by a sequence of mountains.

The spacecraft surrounded the Moon, and the moment the boy saw himself on its well-known dark side, he began to look with attention at every detail. Suddenly, the ship came to a stop and landed on the light side of the Moon. After landing, Nicholas felt his body and soul relax a bit.

His dream had come true at last, and it looked as if it would be far better than everything he had read in books and magazines.

For the first time in his life, he was able to watch the immensity of the Cosmos up close. He glanced at the Sun and admired its brightness; he stared at the planets in our solar system and at its distant stars. Everything was marvelous.

He was excited with the possibility of being the first human being to see the stars from such an extraordinary perspective: from the inside of a spaceship furnished with high levels of technology. What he didn't know was if he would be alive to tell his story to the world.

Then, he put his wonder aside, turned away from Zara and started thinking about the purpose of that journey.

"What do these ETs want from a person such as me, a mere student with no links to scientific or technological researches? I wonder if they are telling the truth or if they intend to dissect me like humans do with guineas pigs."

Nick looked at his love and searched her eyes for the truth; he needed to solve many questions that were making him confused. She smiled in a soft manner, as if reading his thoughts. Nicholas smiled back, although deep inside he was scared and suspicious.

Sivoc soon came close and started to talk about the purpose of the mission.

"Nicholas, I know the way we approached you seemed rather strange, let alone the fact that we brought you to the spacecraft with no further explanations. But we have a situation here: we need you to help us solve a serious issue in our planet."

"How can I be helpful to creatures with such advanced technology?"

The young man couldn't understand anything. All that mystery made no sense to him. He had always dreamed of seeing the universe in person, but traveling to other galaxy had never been in his plans, even more with people he barely knew. As for Zara, he did not know if she was the woman, he had thought she was. He felt betrayed, disappointed. He didn't see how true her feelings for him were.

"Several ancestors of ours have already landed on Earth", Drako cut in. "We have information that your planet's governments tried to imprison them in order to get data about us, our knowledge, and technologies, which could represent an improvement in the world's race for economy and weapons. That explains our fear to have an open and direct contact with you. Above all, we are here in a mission: to protect our home. And only you can help us."

That was when the earthling got mixed up.

"How could I be successful in protecting their planet? They have plenty of knowledge. Much more than I do, for sure."

While the boy seemed to be lost in his own thoughts, something went on between Sivoc and Zara. She looked at the Commander, because she had received a message in her mind.

"Zara, we should talk straight to Nicholas. He must trust us. And the truth about our mission will show him that our own intentions are the best of all, and that we act in good faith. First, we must tell him about our main objective, then we'll tell him the whole story since the beginning, so that our guest understands better why we're here, as well as the links we have with his planet. Moreover, we know he's under risk. There's another ship from planet Life coming after him.

It must be getting nearby now, and they won't be compassionate to the boy."

The redhead moved closer to her love.

"We live in about the 641° Century, according to your age's chronology, Nick. We're able to travel through time due to the advances in the technology of our era. We have found several space-time bridges, which the physicists of your planet call wormholes. That's how we fast cover big distances among our galaxies."

Those moments inside the spaceship felt like hours. It seemed as if the clocks had stopped. Nicholas was feeling more comfortable, though. It might have been the effect of the quality of the oxygen that he was breathing, which made him feel as if everything that was happening around him didn't matter.

That was a unique experience for him. He couldn't understand clearly what was going on, but all his attention was on the pieces of knowledge he was getting. After such startling discoveries, he needed to learn more.

"For a long while, beings from our planet have come to Earth in order to extend life as much as possible and make it better there. Many actions have been taken in order to help your people, who are still on the path to evolution.

Thus, we stop you from taking catastrophic measures that could also represent our end. At the same time, we cannot change the past by creating temporal paradoxes that may cause any harm to the lives of human beings of the future. We do a type of work based on observation, interfering preventively in the present. If humanity takes the path to destruction, we will redirect it to self-preservation."

Nicholas' facial expression was one of pure panic; he felt sick, on the verge of fainting. It was too much information for a single guy.

"The actual truth is that we are humanity in the future." Zara said.

Chapter 5

Nicholas didn't know very well what was going on, and his face showed concern because of so many revelations. It was too much information for one single mind! He was confused with everything he had heard so far. Zara invited him to sit down.

"How could you open gaps in the time, and how could you find the wormholes? What will humans be like in the future? Ah, how about the name of the planet: Life? Why wasn't the name Earth maintained, even if it's in another galaxy?" He asked after resting and recovering himself.

"Keep calm, Nick, please. We'll tell you everything soon", the girl said again.

"How can I keep calm among so many discoveries? I wonder if I am going nuts, and this place is a fricking mental institution..."

The boy wanted answers for all those questions, but one of them still lingered insistently in his mind: why in the world had he been taken? What was so special about him, a mere student, and a star admirer?

The spaceship's crew exchanged glances. Nicholas had his eyes fixed on Sivoc, waiting for the answers they had promised him, and trying to understand what was asked of him.

"In truth, you are gifted with an immune system which is very different from the other human beings'", Sivoc told him. "And that particularity of yours turned you into a subject of study in the future."

The young man was astonished with such a revelation.

"What do you mean by 'different from other human beings?'"

"All information about you, kept on the medical files and then shared on the web, made you known as the bearer of the most powerful antibodies of all people on Earth." The Commander went on with explanations while Nick could barely take his eyes off him, eager for more answers. "Your blood has an amazing sequence of lymphocytes in its composition that has never been seen in any other being. Lymphocytes N. These cells make you immunologically strong against infections and all types of disease."

"Things are starting to make some sense now," Nicholas thought. In fact, while many of his friends got colds and other mild diseases such as virus infections during childhood and adolescence, he had maintained himself healthy. Sometimes he had pretended to be ill so that he could miss one or another day of class, but in fact he had never been sick. His mother used to take him to the doctors for routine visits and the results always tested negative for all illnesses. He had taken his shots against many diseases like any other child, but had never even caught a mild flu. Lorena used to listen to other mothers complain about their children's pharyngitis and colds, and sometimes got embarrassed because she had nothing to say about her son. She was afraid of telling them that her kid had never been sick and end up having her boy turned into a subject of study by doctors who might want take him to some laboratories elsewhere. Better leave things the way they were and Nick healthy as he had always been.

"Scientists from the Future realized that a sort of genetic mutation had taken place in your defense cells, which would explain how your body could develop this power of healing."

"I think I already know what they want to do with me. I'm sure they're planning on doing some experiments with my blood in their planet! They're planning to dissect my body the same way scientists do on Earth with guinea pigs. I don't want to travel with them. I must find a way to get out of here. I just can't lose my family! But how am I going to do that?"

Zara could feel her lover's agony and asked Sivoc to keep persuading him.

"Sivoc, please, tell Nick about our reasons to take him with us. He's a good man and will realize we are telling the truth."

"We found you due to a request made by the governor of planet Life, King Zador II. Princess Isadora, his daughter, was affected by a rare disease caused by a virus. Not even the most powerful and modern medications available on our kingdom were enough to cure her. However, we already knew about you and about lymphocytes N. The cells were named after you, Nicholas. And since we had enough technology expertise to go back in the past through the space-time gap and warp drive engines, the solution would be to reach you: the human being whose defense cells are the strongest of all. Not even in our time we have somebody as strong as you are."

"But with so much technology and scientific evolution, wouldn't there be a way to find a cure? Did they need to look for a simple student of the past like me?"

"Pathogenic life forms evolve just as we do. Look at your planet. As much as scientists manage to create antibiotics, vaccines and serums, there are always some diseases that catch everyone by surprise. In this way, pandemics destroy thousands of lives. There will always be unknown diseases. But you are unique and we don't have time to wait for a cure. Please!"

In a sudden, the earthling realized the importance of this mission: he could help someone. He found he was special, although he hadn't figured out how special he was yet. He still feared what those creatures could want from him, in fact. He didn't want to undergo several painful experiences. He wanted to save someone's life, but to what extent could he lose his own?

"King Zador will be very thankful to anyone who can help heal his daughter, and a very generous prize will be offered to the one who does it. Therefore, he requested that his counselors set up two groups to travel back in time, to the Terrestrial past, to find you. The team I'm in charge of was chosen by Counselor Kenan, a man who's very loyal to the king. He chose us due to our scientific and technological knowledge. We were given the spaceship Science, this one we are in now." Sivoc opened his arms, making Nick's eyes sweep the place.

"The other task force was chosen by Mirov, another royal counselor, but one that makes use of military force. Although he enjoys the king's trust, we have received information that he plans to betray the king and carry out a coup d'etat, so we don't trust him. They were given the spaceship Star Hunter, which is led by a very skilled and ambitious man. Merko's willing to do everything he can to accomplish his goals. By good luck, his ship needed to be fixed, so we were able to take off in advance and find you before they did. Our goal is simple, Nicholas: we want to take you to our planet so that you can donate a small number of your bone marrow cells. They are our last hope of healing the princess."

The young man was astonished with what had been just revealed to him.

"So, I'm not supposed to serve as a guinea pig? All they need is a donation of cells. Even so, I can't go. I have to stay with my family. I'm the one who can protect Sophia and my mom. I won't go, no doubt. Since I have a choice, I'm going to ask them to take me back home", he thought.

While the boy was absorbed by his thoughts, Commander Sivoc went on with his explanation.

"The real problem is that, if the Princess dies, the King will have no heir. And the rules in our planet are clear: in case of no heir, the new governor must be chosen among the members of the Council. That's why Mirov wanted to form a task force so much, as a way to enhance his prestige. On top of that, we also fear that Star Hunter's crew real intention may be to eliminate you, Nicholas, and thus destroy our last chance to save the little girl. That is why we are asking you to come with us and, if you do, we'll be able to protect you and guarantee our future Queen's survival."

Zara took the opportunity and said some words to try to build an argument that could persuade Nick to go with them.

"The virus that infected Isadora seems to be a very aggressive mutant of the same kind that has taken her mother's life. It attacks the blood cells and can't be defeated by any of the traditional procedures known by our doctors. The child has been suffering from anemia and getting weaker as days go by. We believe that the lymphocytes from your bone marrow will be able to cure her, because they are strong and might resist the virus."

The earthling was still thinking about what to do.

"If something like that happened to my sister, I'd help her at once. I wonder how her father feels. If it happened to a member of my family, I'd fully appreciate if somebody volunteered to heal them. Besides, this 'Merko' wants me dead, and, according to what they said, he's pretty dangerous. Meanwhile, if I go back to Earth, I'll put the lives of those I love at risk. These aliens here are the ones who can protect me now. Yep. I'll have to go with them. There's nothing else I can do."

Although under emotional pressure, Nicholas felt immense pleasure for being able to help healing Isadora. He was afraid at first, regarding what those people would want to do with him, but now that he knew everything was about making a person well - and he'd just have to do a mere donation -, he couldn't deny the request. The feeling of being able to save a life was unique, and he could barely wait for the moment to show himself useful. Zara was showing him not just a different world, but also a way to become a better human being.

"What is she like?" The young man knew there were more relevant questions to be asked, all of them scrambled inside his mind, but that was the one which came out of his mouth.

"She's a nice seven-year-old girl, with an angelic face. She loves to play and she strongly believes she'll find the cure to her illness", the woman said. "So, Nick, are you coming with us? Please, help us save our Princess," she asked.

After being told about the real purpose of his trip, the boy thought about how good it would be to help saving someone, a child of all people. Thus, he had already made his decision. So little was asked of him, it would be a pleasure to help healing Isadora. Besides, even if he wanted to get out of there very much, he couldn't do it, and if he did, he'd be in serious danger with Mirov's task force on his trail in order to get rid of him.

"As far as I'm concerned, she'll be okay. I will do my best for her," the earthling said, altruistically. "But you must promise me that you'll bring me back safe and sound. I need to take care of my mom and sister. I'm the last person they have left in their lives and I can't be far away from them."

"We'll bring you back. It's a promise."

"I wanted to ask you one more thing."

"Go ahead."

"My friend Sanches... I'd like him to go with me very much. I think he could help us on this mission somehow."

Tibor overheard the conversation and interceded.

"I'll get this boy myself."

"Can I go too?" Nicholas asked.

"Yes, young man. You can show me where to find your friend. I'll take Drako with me to help us."

"It'll be nice to take a walk on solid ground." Drako cheered as Sivoc and Zara watched.

Relaxed after hearing Zara promise she would take him back home, Nick thought next to Sanches he would live the greatest adventure of his life, and as soon as it was finished, he would go back to Earth to live with his family again.

While lost in his thoughts, a little dog-shaped robot came up by his feet.

"What's this?" Nicholas asked, with a smile full of surprise, and finding everything fantastic. Now that most of his fears had vanished, he was relaxed, and his curiosity was at the top. The presence of the robot helped to lighten up the atmosphere that was a bit tense due to the risks the princess was under. "I was surprised with this thing rubbing against me."

"In our planet, we have some robots that are reproductions of old puppies. They're something similar to companions, friends, and sometimes even weapons. This is Wolfie. Sometimes it goes along with us in some missions, but it usually stays here looking after the ship and not allowing strangers to get in."

"It's rubbing his head against my leg. I think it likes me," the earthling said, stroking the little robot on the head as if he was caressing some little dog on his city.

"Unfortunately, we couldn't save all terrestrial animals. Those that weren't able to escape extinction, we could clone, using DNA and robotic technology, and thus creating bionic beings with some of the extinct animal's characteristics. Wolfie inherited the gene responsible for the affection we see in most dogs on Earth. Don't let yourself be fooled, though: its eyes shoot high-precision and long-reach laser rays. It also has a nose with high levels of specialization and infra and ultra-sonorous hearing. It may be very helpful in some missions. It's a good buddy, but a very useful machine as well."

Without any delay, Nicholas stepped away from Wolfie, thinking it was better not to play with it. Back home, pets were less dangerous than they were there, without question. Zara smiled, reading his mind.

Nick was more relaxed now and happy with the possibility of helping those people. And the robot made him sure he had a lot to learn with that task force. He would donate some cells to save a child, and in return he would get not just the satisfaction of doing good to another person, but also the opportunity to learn a lot too.

Meanwhile, Captain Merko's ship prepared to leave planet Life on a mission to capture the boy. Sivoc's task force needed a plan...

Chapter 6

Sivoc knew they could not be there for long. Danger peeked at them in more than one form, and it was necessary to think of a safe place for them. Earth's governments were avid to capture them with eyes fixed on their technological developments.

While Sivoc, Drako and Tibor tried to find the best strategy to protect themselves, Nicholas and Zara kept aside, since the subject was beyond their sphere.

"Nick, I think we should go to the medical room. I want to check you up since you felt dizzy in the ship a while ago. As you know, I'm the doctor in charge here."

"Ok, but you'll have to show me the way. I'm lost here."

They left through a door on the wall. The earthling saw a hallway with white bulbs on the ceiling and on the floor showing the path to be followed. Some blue lights bathed the walls made of glass, from where it was possible to watch the Cosmos.

The hallways were long and there were crossings that led to places he couldn't even imagine. The woman stood by a door and it opened at once.

They got to the Medical Center. It had white walls and ten beds, placed side by side. Two nurses, both with human features, worked there, and left the room as soon as the girl looked at them. She wanted to talk to her love privately, and that's why she had asked him to go with her to that room.

"So, doctor Zara, are you examining me? Yesterday you were a student like me at the university. Now, you are the doctor in charge in this ship... Things aren't always what they seem to be, huh?"

"Nick, I know you aren't feeling well," she looked down looking for words. "If I were in your shoes, I'm sure I would feel dizzy too. You, terrestrials, don't even think there's life somewhere other than Earth and I'm sure it will still take some time for you to believe in it, but... I need to tell you that, regarding you and me..."

Nicholas looked at her, anxiety filling his body.

"Everything I told you I felt when we were together was true, and I'd do everything again to be by your side. I've never felt anything like that in my entire existence and I'm grateful to you for letting me understand what love is about. Love, something so special and that few people can experience during their lifetime."

"Zara, I'm sorry, but I'm not sure what to believe in anymore."

The young man wasn't sure if what the woman was saying was true or not. He couldn't even tell if it was Zara herself the person he was seeing there, at that exact moment. However, that mouth of hers moving in slow motion didn't cease to fascinate him. That red hair, hanging over her forehead, and her personality, typical of a woman who knows quite well what she wants; those were things every young man always searched for.

The earthling watched her white clothes, tight over her body and showing her perfect frame. In his opinion, the doctor had no flaws, and that's why it was so hard to resist her. She was clever, beautiful and sexy, things that he had always wanted to find in a woman. She had characteristics that he couldn't find in anyone else. On top of that, there was his favorite perfume too: the scent of jasmine that she wore at the perfect dose.

That's why, after hearing her words of love, Nicholas went close to her and, shy as he was, he kissed the woman, trying to make up for the lost time and missing their dates in the shack. He got lost in her honey lips.

"Nick, my love, trust me. I'll take care of you. I have many things to tell you, but I'll do it at the right time."

"Zara, you're the best thing that has happened in my life. I still don't know who you are in fact, but I decided to let my instincts lead me and I hope they're right."

As soon as they made up, they went back to the bridge where the others talked. Feeling better with each other, they smiled as if they shared a secret.

When they got there, they realized the crew had already found a solution to protect the boy. It was time now to answer his questions. The doctor was aware of the commander's desire to tell the young man about all the mutations humanity had undergone through times, the way they had evolved, in what it had resulted in the future and other issues such as the name of the planet and the reason they had gone to other galaxies.

"I'm very glad you've agreed to help us. And I want to tell you about the evolution of human beings. Would you like to listen to it?"

The earthling' eyes brightened with the perspective to learn more.

"Oh, please, I'd love to learn more about what has happened. I think, though, that human beings haven't changed much, since I don't see many changes on you."

Sivoc smiled when he heard Nicholas' mistaken words. They were funny, but they made perfect sense, because he had not seen the crew's real physical appearance yet.

"That's not quite right," the commander said. "But I'll tell you the story since the beginning. First, I have to tell you that we chose the name of the planet we colonized in the future based on what we most value in the world: life. Earth had already been devastated in the past due to the environmental degradation, pandemics and by the wars that caused food and water shortage. We didn't want to remember such a sad event of the history of humanity that had put an end to billions of lives." He took a deep breath and went on. "That sphere you saw in the spaceship's hologram is planet Life, in our galaxy, Andromeda. We control it from our ship."

Things started to make sense in the boy's mind.

"Going back to your species' evolution process, I can tell you that we have detailed data on the biologic mechanisms of all species from your planet. Thus, there is no need for us to make experiments with you or other beings. When we are on a mission, our main goal is to collect genes to restore extinct species through the process of cloning. Science ship has a wide database with most of terrestrial genome. I think it's worth it to talk a bit about how we developed from the modern Homo sapiens. As you may know, the human brain has a surprising capacity of storing data. With the development of I. T. and the increase of knowledge, brain development was accelerated due to the urgent need for keeping up with the innovations of each generation."

Nicholas listened to what the commander said and felt immersed in a fantastic and unknown world. The more time passed by, the more interested he was.

"Thus, inventions and technology increased exponentially and the human mind developed quicker. These two facts together caused the brain's increase, and consequently, the skull's, in a different scale from the rest of the body. Also, due to the changes on the food patterns that started two centuries ago in your time, the jaws mutated because of soft and industrialized foods that didn't need to be chewed anymore. With no chewing, the last teeth of each series of the dental arch, the incisor teeth, molar teeth, and premolar teeth faded, becoming just remnants of what they used to be. In other words, many genetic mutations took place according to the environment, for thousands and thousands of years."

The boy had never heard such a thing in all his short life.

"What is Sivoc talking about? Will we be big-headed and with a small chin?"

Making use of his telepathic abilities, the commandant realized the boy had understood beyond doubt how his species' evolution had taken place. And Zara decided to go on with the explanation by telepathy too.

"Your conclusion regarding the future is right, Nick. That's why I said we are the future of the humanity."

Nicholas, who was paying attention to the captain's words, turned his eyes to his beloved and listened attentively to her.

"Zara, are you reading my mind and talking to me through telepathy? That is just fantastic! I'd love to be able to do it too." The young man was impressed with that ability of hers, but he was confused too. "I just can't understand. How can you guys be so developed when you share the same appearance of the people I know?"

"Nick, telepathy is something usual where we live. We all make careful use of it. However, we use it with caution and we've learned how to block thoughts' reading when we don't want people to read them."

"Gosh! I can't believe that... It's amazing!

She smiled and started to tell him telepathically how men had devastated the terrestrial ecosystem.

"Well, picking up from where we left off, we all know that the star around which the Earth spins is still going to last something around six billion years. To guarantee the preservation of the planet, though, it's necessary for human beings to be aware of the importance of renovating Earth's ecosystem. In some decades, men will start to use alternative energy sources more frequently because there won't be any possibilities to compensate the lack of petroleum energy sources. Then, men will control solar energy and atomic nuclear fusion technology, which will allow a multiplicity of energy sources and an increase of radiation. However, with the ineffectiveness of radioactive control methods, mainly caused by countries which will make use of that method without enough expertise, there will be more damage on the ozone layer. Consequently, a bigger amount of solar radiation will reach the atmosphere and change the weather's conditions drastically. Moreover, the exponential increase of people in the world will cause so many wars for food and water that Earth will become hard to live on, and there will be a search for other places that can be home to our species. Besides that, the use of glass domes filled with filtered oxygen and extra protection against solar and cosmic radiation will be necessary. Consequently, the partially closed system that heats and moisturizes the air, which we call nasal cavities, will be extinct, causing nasal atrophy and consequently reducing our noses to two small holes."

Nicholas tried to imagine how human beings would look in the future, but that wasn't an easy task. And Zara had even more to tell him.

"Vision through two eyes also underwent changes. When men finally started living in outer space, their vision had to adapt to their new way of life, improving deepness perception in order to see better and reach objects that are far away. This resulted in an increase of size and in an increase of space between the eyes. As for the fingers, they shrunk due to the change most productive activities have gone through, once the robotization of the means of production ceased all manual work. As generations went by, finger functions lost their importance. Hands have just three fingers now, and no nails. After all, for many years, humanity has had no need for claws. Also, due to the use of telepathy for communication purposes, outer ears have withered away and our inner ears reduced up to small holes, just like it happened to our noses."

He imagined himself with the features described and was afraid of the possibility of all of that being true. If he told his peers at university everything he had just heard, he might be considered crazy. Nobody would believe him, even though he was telling the truth. He also realized that the girl he had fallen in love with couldn't be as beautiful as she seemed to be and so similar to terrestrial girls. Nick was curious to see how those people were in their real shape.

Zara gazed at the central control panel, and a hologram came in front of them showing her beloved how they looked like in the future. The boy was shocked when he realized that human beings of the future were the extraterrestrials we fear so much now.

With eyes wide open, he felt scared.

Chapter 7

While Zara and Nicholas talked about the evolution of humanity, the crew concluded that the best option was to go back to his country and hide there.

Drako told the commandant:

"Captain Sivoc, the ideal moment to form a space-time passage will be in a few weeks. The path's an intergalactic bridge near the Calisto moon, from Jupiter, which will take us straight to our solar system. To cross it, though, we must leave here. There won't be enough time to wait where we are now."

"Terrestrial radars can see us, and so can Captain Merko's enemy spaceship, which is going to Earth. They can intercept us with ease from the battlecruiser even if we hide the ship Science in some neighboring planet." Sivoc said.

"There, we can infiltrate ourselves among human beings and it'll be easier for us not to be seen. We'll live a normal life while we wait for the day of our departure. The spacecraft can be hidden in the oceans, which are wide, and radars will have difficulty finding us if we hide the ship near deep rocks. It's going to be hard even for Star Hunter ship. When Captain Merko gets there and realizes that the boy is with us, he'll come after us like night comes after the day", Drako complemented.

"Drako, put the spaceship on invisible mode now that we aren't under any risk. We must find shelter for Science spacecraft in the deepness of the sea, out of the reach for terrestrial radars and hidden from our enemy", the captain ordered.

"Yes, Captain. I'll forward latitude and longitude coordinates to our X2 computer. We'll search for a safe place to land in the Atlantic Ocean, close to Tampico, a city in the Gulf of Mexico."

The order of landing on Earth was spread throughout the whole vehicle, even in the engine room where Sargent Amaya, the officer in charge, and her peer Pewse talked to each other.

"Pewse, do you think it is possible for us to fight Captain Merko's spacecraft? I've heard Star Hunter is unbeatable, equipped with heavy artillery and ready to destroy the enemy, no matter who it is."

"That would be a kind of suicide", said the Sargent. "Maybe with three ships together from our planet we could be able to fight them."

"The commander's order says we should hide from them and wait for the right moment to go back to Life", Amaya answered.

"I have no doubt that is the best choice."

Sivoc's crew would try to outwit Captain Merko until they felt it was the right moment to go back to the planet they came from. After concluding about what would be the best way to accomplish the mission, each member of the crew went back to their position. Sivoc, however, moved towards Nicholas in order to talk to him. First, he talked mentally to Zara.

"How about we show ourselves the way we are in truth to our visitor?"

"I don't know, Commander. He might be frightened by our true appearance. Although we are humans too, the genetic mutations we went through are as significant as those suffered by the Homo sapiens from when they were Australopithecus. At the same time, though, we are taking the boy to our planet. Therefore, I think Nicholas should know how we are. He'll have to face reality one way or the other", the woman said, worried about her lover's possible reactions.

"Yes, he has to know," the captain answered.

Deep in her heart, Zara wanted to be with Nick, even if it was a remote possibility. Sivoc turned to the boy.

"Are you ready to see us the way we actually are, Nicholas?"

Nick nodded in agreement. He was nervous. Seeing his love in her human shape was enough for him.

Telepathically, the Commander asked all of them to abandon their earthling shapes. They touched the bracelets they wore on their wrists and revealed their real form. Nicholas saw them squirm as if in pain during the transformation.

Seconds later, after watching them for a while, Nick gazed at the redhead and had mixed feelings.

"Yeah, the love of my life isn't the way I thought she was, and that's a fact... But she is so sweet. And she's also a clever woman who works to save lives. I can see in her eyes how much she likes me and I also love her because of the special person she is. In her human shape, she is so beautiful and affectionate! Someone that, if she lived with me on Earth, could make me happier, and I would also be the guy with the most special girlfriend in the Universe."

Nick was astonished when he saw those people with the same shape, he had seen on the hologram a while ago, but that was the plain truth. At the same moment, he was also uncertain about his own feelings. Could he love a woman who belonged to the future? Moreover, could he love a woman with such an appearance?

In his mind, the earthling made a comparison: "To have a date with a woman from the future, which is what's happening now, would be the same as a Homo sapiens dating an

Australopithecus like Lucy in the past. A very weird situation, to say the least."

Zara realized Nick's disappointment when he saw her peers' faces. She was sad and telepathically asked them all to go back to their earthling forms. She felt something new for that terrestrial, a kind of emotion that she had never felt before. When she took the form of the beautiful woman Nick had fallen in love with, she saw him smile the same way he had smiled when she had first met him at the university. Seeing her in his species' shape gave him some hope as to extending his love for her.

"I'm too different from Nicholas in spite of the fact that we are both humans. The consequences of having a relationship with someone from the past would be unpredictable but, at the same time, I love him so much! Since the first moment I saw him. I just don't know what to do. It may be better not to dream about the impossible."

The young man was amazed with the use of technology for transmutation and wondered if it would be possible for him make use of it and be whoever he wanted to be. That was unbelievable!

Sivoc went on with his explanation:

"As I believe you have already seen at university, there is a link between space and time. When you travel from a place to another, time changes according to the distance you have crossed. The space-time web is deformed when other celestial body, with enough mass to cause such a deformation, settles itself on it, and the warp that is formed results in gravity. From that knowledge, scientists could produce propulsion engines for these warps, contracting the space in front of the ship and expanding the space left behind. We also travel through wormholes that are formed from gravitational space-time warps, which can open tunnels among distant galaxies. Besides that, we make use of artificial gravity that allows us to travel comfortably through the Universe."

Being a devoted student of Physics, Nicholas loved everything related to time travel, life on other planets, the Theory of Relativity, energy sources and artificial gravity. For him, listening to all of that was wonderful.

Zara showed him the galaxy where they lived on the virtual screen with enthusiasm. She pointed her finger at her home, which was at a similar distance to their star to that between our Earth and the Sun. That was Life, the place where all of them lived.

She accessed some new images and the boy could realize that planet Life had some things in common with Earth, as for example, plenty of water and some green areas with several types of forests.

"Human beings got to our galaxy after they had settled colonies on many natural satellites and other planets. Their first home was the Moon. Due to the Environmental degradation and the world on the verge of destruction, the USA, as well as some eastern countries got together to create the first artificial biome in Universe. Another colony was settled in Mars. Then, other places were explored, and with the development of technology, men also reached the frontiers of the Milky Way. At last, by figuring out how to travel across the wormholes, they found the Planet where we live now, in Andromeda Galaxy. It's a spiral galaxy and is placed 2.9 million light-years away from the solar system to which Earth belongs to", the doctor said. "It's the spiral galaxy closest to the Milky Way, and it was named after the Andromeda Constellation, where it is placed. Andromeda is also called Messier 31 and has several stars twice the galaxy we are in now."

"But, Zara, how was it possible to unite countries with so many diverse concerns when you told me there were a lot of wars for food and water?"

"Spatial programs are too expensive for one country alone to afford. Those countries got together in order to get better outcomes for human beings. If they didn't do that, it would result in the extinction of mankind. Our species' instinct of survival was the most important ingredient to the recipe of world union. Planet Life was the best place we found, for there we could produce water from huge masses of ice and heat the environment with vast sources of energy captured from nuclear fusion and from the use of special light ab-sorption panels to convert solar energy into electricity. That caused a cycle of evaporation of water that, in addition to the harvest of a genetically modified forest, started a continuous photosynthesis that provided oxygen for the atmosphere. The planet's convenient position regarding the sun helped, too. We were able to save some species, both animal and plant's, which were taken with us to our trips through the Universe. We also have several domestic animals that are different from the ones you know today, because they have under-gone genetic mutations during their evolution process. With a quite diverse DNA database, we could clone many extinct species and recover a significant amount of the biodiversity that had been destroyed," said Zara, who now was not just the beautiful woman Nick had met one day in the classroom of the university, but someone that attracted him more and more.

"Everything you are saying sounds like a dream to me. Despite all the science and technology, we have nowadays, it is very hard to put humans together to save the planet. Their concerns diverge, and even actions like saving children who flee from war don't seem to be possible for them. It seems that mankind evolves, but their selfishness is the same it used to be in the Dark Age. I believe that what you are saying is the most absolute truth. Just watch the news and you'll see the world still has many issues with no solution."

While they talked, X2 Computer led the ship through the terrestrial atmosphere. Drako monitored a communication that came from an artificial base settled by men in order to defend the globe. It was called Multination Orbital Station and, at that moment, its radars identified the presence of an UFO. Drako accessed the conversation that took place on Earth.

"Attention, Spatial Mission on Earth: spaceship seen on the surroundings of the Northern area of the planet. Any jet fighters in the area?" Asked the French Commander Raunot in charge of the Station.

The UFO was Science ship and, once more, Nicholas' life was in danger.

Chapter 8

Everyone was scared in the Multination Orbital Station. It was located on Earth's low orbit, some 400 miles in height, where it was able to exchange information with the terrestrial officers. It was the first time that team identified a UFO. A signal had been sent to all military bases settled in the countries' members of the Spatial Planet Program. Alert level: maximum.

At the ground center of command in Houston, the warning sounds made everyone agitated. The military soldiers got equipped for a possible ground offensive. The fuss among the soldiers and the support groups was significant, so unusual was the attack. The Russian Operation Center volunteered to help monitoring the attack, and the Chinese Spatial Program was ready for any emergency.

From the control room, the French commander listened to answers to his call.

"Loud and clear, Orbital Spatial Command. European Command of the Spatial Mission in Germany speaking. We have two jet fighters waiting to intercept the attack. Waiting for permission to shoot", Ramon Fritz answered.

"Hello. Houston? Anybody there? Imminent danger of invasion by alien spaceship. Over." Raunot tried to communicate with the American in-chief of the Spatial Mission.

"Houston speaking. Roger. Military Command on alert," General Stheford answered from the base.

"Two F16s ready to shoot near Alaska. They're on the way, Sir", Colonel Smith, from the American Command, said.

"Try to capture the ship and its crew by contacting them first. That would be a landmark in Human History. If they answer with weapons, you have permission to destroy the vehicle", Raunot ordered.

"Copy. We'll do as you say." Fritz answered.

"Yes, Sir Wilco." Smith affirmed.

The alarms went off, cutting through the air around the alien spacecraft. The spaceship Science crew was alert. Drako warned Sivoc right away.

"Captain, we've been identified by human radars. Four jet fighters are coming toward us. We must take off as soon as possible; otherwise, we'll be forced to shoot them, and it could compromise our objective."

"Take us to the orbit of Jupiter. We'll be invisible there." Sivoc ordered.

In an ultra-high speed, they left the planet's orbit and got to Jupiter, crossing the Asteroid Belt and stationing next to the Ganymede Moon.

On Earth, the German Command returned the Orbital Station's call.

"The UFO has just vanished from our radars. Can you see anything?"

"Negative, Fritz. I'll ask the other Commands to try to find it", the leader of the Multination Orbital Station spoke.

"Smith speaking. I've also lost the target. Mission aborted."

A protocol was filed in Houston, and the officer in charge of extraterrestrial issues typed the report. He checked the label on the letterhead that read:

CONFIDENTIAL MATTER

* * *

"What happened, Drako? How could human radars detect us? That's not possible!" Sivoc asked as soon as things calmed down.

"Captain, X2 scanned our Defense Systems and found a small failure in our antiradar shields. It's being fixed now."

"Let me know as soon as it finishes it. We must hide from Merko's ship. We won't have the same luck we had with humans. Human airships do not trespass the terrestrial atmospheric layer, but our spaceships can go anywhere in the Universe."

"Yes, Sir."

As soon as the spacecraft was ready, the shields were activated and it went back into the atmosphere. This time, without being detected by the radars. When it was near the Gulf of Mexico, the vehicle dove into the ocean.

"What was that? I heard a kind of buzz," Nicholas said.

"We've just gotten into the open sea," Zara told him. "It's one of our favorite places to hide, since there are many rocks that block any trace of our presence."

Nicholas looked through the glass of the control room. He saw some turtles, dolphins, and fish. Seeing the marine fauna so close was a splendid view.

"Look at those animals!"

Zara's eyes watered.

"What happened, Zara? Why are you crying?"

"Some years ago, there was an oil leak somewhere near here. The ecological damage was tragic. It's going to take decades for the marine fauna to recover, although we can still see some animals left that provide us with such a beautiful view. It's very sad to see a place as beautiful as Earth being destroyed. Mankind should take care of its homeland, other-wise there will be no place to call their own." Nicholas gave Zara a hug and they both shared her grief.

The ship continued to dive in until it found a safe place to land.

"We have to carry on with our plan", Sivoc said.

"Let's get ready at once", Tibor answered, while Drako checked any possible signal from the enemy's spaceship.

* * *

Meanwhile, Star Hunter ship had already left the central dock of Perfectio, the official capital of Life. From the command room, Captain Merko watched the huge hangar which ceiling had several mirrored stainless-steel domes that closed after the departure. He could also see the entrance of the rectangular base surrounded by a blue light. The transportation vehicles and the spaceships parked all over the base got smaller and smaller as his own flew away. He left the planet behind him; that wonderful image of a blue globe with its yellowish halo that he considered home.

All coordinates had been set in order to get to the wormhole formed by Calisto, Jupiter's Moon, where the gravitational curves between the Andromeda and Milk Way galaxies met. That was the place where the other end of the space-time tunnel was settled. He was eager to accomplish the assignment while Counselor Mirov gave the last instructions from the communication room in the Royal Palace.

"Captain, don't forget to keep in touch with us through my private communication channel. I want you to report all information about the mission to me. The scientific ship is not prepared to accomplish such an errand. If they're attacked by the terrestrial armies, they will be caught."

"Counselor, my team, and I will do everything in our power to bring you the boy safe and sound. No one will keep me from reaching my goals."

"I need the earthling dead or alive. If he dies, I require you to extract his bone marrow in the cryogenic lab. His blood and its special defense cells are everything that matters."

In his extraterrestrial shape, the commander contracted the muscles of his jaw, thinking about his next plans. His physical constitution was tall and strong. Crom, his first officer, watched his brave Captain's concern. In addition to being famous for always accomplishing his goals, Merko was a good soldier and a generous man.

Radof, Mirov's assistant, who stood by his master, was surprised when he heard his last order. Saving the life of the princess was not in his priorities, and he knew that. Aware of his image projected onto the command room hologram, he looked away trying to hide his astonishment.

"I'll keep you informed, Sir. In a few minutes, we'll start moving in warp speed."

"Have a nice journey, Captain. I hope you return with good news."

At the Royal Palace, Counselor Mirov left the Communication Room. He walked along the long hallway until he reached his chambers. Radof was on his heels.

"Come in, you pathetic man", Mirov ordered.

"Excuse me, sir. I heard you talking to the captain, and I know for a fact that the Counselor doesn't want the Princess to live."

"It's obvious, you idiot! But I couldn't tell him the truth, otherwise he would put me in jail in the blink of an eye. I have to make the Commander bring the boy here. But, first, Merko needs to believe my noble intentions. Despite everybody fearing him because of his strength and fame, he is a man of principles. I'll exchange the earthling's bone marrow for another one, and when the girl needs it most, it will be too late. Regarding the King, I also have a perfect plan for him." Mirov said with a smile.

"That's very clever of you, Sir. Nobody will suspect your plan. And having the best man chosen for the mission was a master stroke."

"The Commander never failed. The conviction of accomplishing an honorable assignment will help him reach success. Now, shut up and get the entire communication equipment ready in my chambers so that we can monitor everything."

A while later, the battlecruiser Star Hunter got into the Solar system. Captain Merko's ship went down the atmosphere in high speed. It got to Alaska, where there was an extraterrestrial base inside a mountain. A giant door opened in the middle of the snow, allowing the spaceship to get inside the hiding place. Crom talked to his commander.

"A base here is highly strategic, Sir. We're invisible to the governments' radars and we still have a place to hide and prepare the artillery for the missions. This way, we can aim our attention exclusively at finding the earthling, with no fear regarding our safety."

"We've had many bases hidden all over the globe through all ages. During previous trips, beings from our planet were welcome in places like Machu Picchu and Egypt, and with our technology, we could work together and bring glory and peace to humanity. But now we need to be hidden, because present men want our technology to use it for military purposes, and they would imprison us without second thoughts."

Star Hunter's crew knew nothing about the whereabouts of Sivoc's task force, but they believed that they had already gotten to Earth.

Science ship has not used the terrestrial bases because they would be found with ease by their enemy. Now, it was necessary to seek information about the target, and the team chosen by Mirov, all in their human form, teleported to the city of Los Angeles, in the USA, where the boy they were seeking lived.

They all synchronized the planned coordinates and pressed their bracelets they had on their wrists. It was a teleporting device that synchronized present position and the desired one, allowing the molecules of the one who was to be teleported to be transferred, materializing them anywhere within the places covered by the robot-satellite, launched into orbit around the Earth by the lifeans.

Because of their developed technology, the equipment had a four-foot diameter, which could be considered small compared to terrestrial satellite patterns. That's why it couldn't be detected by radars, since it resembled spatial debris, besides counting on another advantage: its wide range of action that covered all the planet's surfaces.

Crom opened the files that included all data collected from the web.

"Commander, we've found some web files with names, photos and addresses of students that go to College with Nicholas - our target. We can try to get some info from them if we find them."

Merko raised something like a pen that projected a hologram in the air with the material they were using. He touched one of the sides of the image and accessed all conversations Nicholas had had with his friends on social medias in the web, searching anything that could reveal the earthling's whereabouts.

The two men leaned over the files to study which strategy would be better and then, after some discussion, they reached a conclusion.

"We had better split into two groups. One group will search information in the boy's house. His mother might know where he is. The other group will go to his friend's house, Sanches is his name, to try to get some evidence. We'll sift through their friends and relatives. I want to know everything that can reveal his whereabouts." The captain said.

Merko and Crom set off to Nicholas' house in the suburbs. Lorena was at home and Sophia was at school. The two men embodied behind a tree near Nicholas' mother's garden while two other men stood around on guard. Both, disguised as police detectives, dressed up in suits and got false identification credentials. Meanwhile, other three men went to Sanches' house.

Lorena was anxious to hear from her son, who had been missing for a couple of days, which was unusual of him. She had already filled a report at the police office. Nicholas always told her where he would be so that she wouldn't worry about him.

Chapter 9

The neighbor's dog barked incessantly as if it recognized the false police officers. Lorena opened the door, alerted by the barks. As soon as she saw the officer, she thought something bad had happened.

"May I help you?"

For a moment, Merko looked into the woman's eyes and had a sense of recognition. The two of them stood there for a moment, looking at each other, saying nothing. Since they were police officers, she though she may have seen him somewhere else and maybe they had already met before.

"Good morning, ma'am. We came here to talk to you about your son. We've gotten a report telling us the boy is missing. I suppose it was you who called us, and the chief officer asked us to check the case in person. Have you had any information about his whereabouts?"

"No... I thought you would bring me some information about Nicholas. He has been missing for some days and we've been desperate to have some news that could give us any hope to find him."

"Can you inform us the last place your son was seen, before he was considered missing?"

"He was riding his bike. It was on Sunday. He always came back home at the end of the afternoon. But it's been four days and he hasn't come back..."

"Can you tell us the route he used to follow... The places he used to go and the clothes he was wearing the last time he was seen?"

"Sure. Nick loved to follow that road that leads to the park," the mother said, reaching out and pointing towards the road. "He was wearing blue shorts and a white T-shirt with some rock band print on the back."

"Did he tell you anything about anyone he had met that day?"

"He had just started seeing a girl, a freshman at university, and he was quite fallen for her."

"Do you know the girl's name, ma'am?"

"No. Not yet. He has not introduced her to us. I think he wanted to be sure it wasn't just a... Fling."

"Thank you, ma'am. Everything you said was very useful for us. We'll keep you updated about any news we get."

The first officer looked at the captain and raised his eyebrows. The commander read the woman's mind and checked if she had indeed told them everything she knew about her son. She had.

"Thank you, officers, and please, discover where my Nick is... Report me everything you hear. Anything, please."

"We will, ma'am."

Merko and Lorena stood there, staring at each other, as if there was more to say.

"Hey, man! You ok? We must go, now." Crom said.

His friend widened his eyes and got a grip on himself. They both left, keeping in mind that they had to find the boy and accomplish the mission before the princess's life came to an end.

They were also worried about not leaving any traces of their visit on Earth. They knew there was an extraterrestrial investigation team, Alfa-Omega, that could cause them trouble. Crom remembered some stories Merko used to tell him during their journeys, and there was one in which a friend of the commander had died, when in battle with that very same Alfa-Omega along with the captain in that same planet too.

Alfa-Omega was a secret operation commanded by the American government, in charge of investigating any sign of alien beings on Earth and surrounding globes. Nobody knew about it, except for high-ranking officers and the US president himself. Since it was linked to the Pentagon itself, it could always ask for any kind of support from the National Command Forces. Every time it captured any species, its agents used secret military bases in Area 51, in Arizona, for confinement and research.

While Merko and his first officer moved towards the other ETs dressed up as policemen, the latter had an idea.

"Why don't you ask our agent in Planet Life about Sivoc's ship coordinates? There is no better advantage than information. Counselor Mirov told you they are here in the USA. They may be able to locate the spaceship."

"That's not a bad idea. Let's do it as soon as we get back to the base".

His group teleported to their hiding place in Alaska to wait for the others that had teleported to Sanches' house. As soon as they got there, the commander contacted Counselor Mirov.

"Counselor Mirov, I need your help. I'd like to ask you to search for a way to hack the Board of Information Systems and find out where Science ship is. This planet here is too big and I believe they might have hidden the ship in a safe place. In addition to that, we can't waste our time looking for it."

"I'll see what can be done," the counselor said.

Mirov turned the communication screen off and pondered about the matter.

"I have to find a way to learn where their ship is. They must have the boy with them by now, and I'm sure Merko can capture him for me. If he brings me the earthling, I'll get rid of him, and with the Princess and her father dead, I'll have good chances of being the new King. After all, I am the oldest

Counselor of the planet, and the one with best reputation of all."

The captain decided to wait for the other group's contact with Sanches and monitor possible communications between Nicholas and his mother, and between the scientific ship and Life. The commander's purpose was to fulfill the duty he had been assigned to: he wanted to locate Nick to help saving the princess's life, and he knew that Sivoc's task force could have some trouble doing it. That's why he was there: to help and protect the king's self-interest. He just could not imagine he was being used by the mischievous counselor Mirov for a diabolic plan.

The commander of battleship Star Hunter also found it weird that the mission hadn't put his and his rival's teams together.

"Why is Sivoc hiding from me, if we are on Earth sharing the same goals? There is something wrong going on... Anyway, I'll do my best to save little Isadora and bring joy back to my world. But first, I must discover where the young man is! I just can't let the scientific squad fail in their mission. So, I myself will take care of it."

* * *

Sanches was fixing his bike's flat tire and felt guilty when he thought about Nicholas.

"¡Que infierno! I shouldn't have argued with Nick. Now, I don't know where he is and, worst of all, I can't do anything to help him."

Suddenly, he heard a noise and felt an unusual movement in the air, which made him investigate the garage and see three men embodying next to his mother's car. Afraid, he hid behind a bush in his garden like a flash. They were dressed up in black suits with navy blue satin ties. There was no better disguise. As policemen, they would be respected and would also be able to inquire people in their search for relevant information.

"Dear God, what is that? Those men just came up out of the blue. It must be a hallucination..." The boy thought, on the verge of losing his mind, when he saw those three people together.

He was so scared that he almost fell into the bush, and tried not to make any noise that could call their attention.

They moved toward the front door and rang the bell. The young man's mom opened the door. Astonished, her hands started trembling and she stood like a statue as soon as she looked at them.

"¡Hola! ¿Qué sucedió, caballeros detectives?"

They showed her their credentials that were on their pockets.

"Señora, tenemos que hacer algunas preguntas a su hijo Sanches por la desaparición de su amigo Nicholas."

The boy entered his home through the back door and showed up behind his mom. He was too pale, too nervous.

"It's all right, mamá. I'll take care of it now. They might want some news about Nick. Lorena said he has been missing for a couple of days. You can go inside. I got this."

"Si, si, pobre muchacho! Está bien, voy a entrar."

"How could those men appear out of the blue? That was all very weird." The young man's main worry now was to protect his mother and get her out of that situation which seemed dangerous and unusual.

"I apologize for my mom. When she gets nervous, she just can't speak English at all. She babbles in Spanish, which is her native language. By the way, I realized that's not a problem for you, for you speak our language too."

"That's okay, boy. You are a friend of Nicholas,' huh? The missing guy. His mother filed a report at the Police Station and we are investigating his case. We're here to get some more information about him, anything you remember."

"I know nothing about him. It has been days since we last saw each other."

The E.T.s exchanged looks and communicated telepathically.

"The specimen is lying. He saw us teleporting in the garage! I could read his mind!"

"There's no alternative other than taking him with us. Otherwise, he will look for the authorities and cause us many problems. Plus, if we kidnap him, he'll be with us and won't be able to tell anyone about our visit here."

The young man watched those people who stared quiet at each other, and he secretly desired they went away. He didn't have a clue about the trap he had fallen into.

One of them took a stunning gun from under his suit and shot him. The boy got motionless in an instant. Then, the men grabbed him by the arm and took him away.

Some minutes later, his mother went after her son, who was taking too long to come in.

"¡Que raro! Sanches, es dónde? Debe de haber ido a comprar algo o salir con una chica en el barrio."

The extraterrestrials showed up with the young man in the Command room. In his extraterrestrial form, Merko turned around when he noticed their presence, and asked in surprise:

"What's the meaning of this?"

The earthling tried to stand up straight after being teleported. He looked around, dazzled by the amazing technology he hadn't thought possible outside of Sci-Fi movies, but when he saw Merko in his alien form, he got so scared that he fainted and fell to the ground.

Chapter 10

While **Nicholas** got amazed with everything happening around, Zara was worried about him. She knew that if they were caught by Merko, her beloved one's destiny would be uncertain. The famous captain was working for counselor Mirov and she, as well as all her team, was suspicious of his real purposes. The woman was also attracted by Nick's beauty and kindness, and taking him safe to her planet, following the king's and counselor Kenan's orders was everything she wanted. She had never felt so much affection for anyone else before, because she always tried to keep entirely focused on her missions, but this time it was different: her feelings were too strong to be put aside.

The doctor had collected all possible data about the earthling: all his medical reports and the strength of his lymphocytes N. She had studied him before making the first contact. Even when she was still in planet Life, she had learnt to admire him, and now she was living reality. She knew the boy had never dated before, and every time he met a girl, he liked to talk about the stars and to include some scientific explanations about them, which made the girls end up letting him talk to himself.

As for the E.T., she too had some issues regarding men from her planet. When they flirted with her, she soon checked their mind and heart to see if she could find anything that could attract her and, most of the time, she realized they were too superficial in the matter of love.

She and the boy, though, were very much alike, despite their differences.

* * *

Drako contacted counselor Kenan, who was in charge of the scientific team's mission commanded by Sivoc, and was told that commander Merko had already arrived at Los Angeles.

"Commander, Star Hunter ship is already on Earth and the Captain, along with all his crew, is searching de city of Los Angeles for the boy. What should we do?" Drako reported to his commander.

"Sooner or later, he'll find out where our ship is. We must find a way of hiding somewhere else, somewhere non-suspicious. As for the spaceship itself, there's no way we can hide it from Merko."

Aware of the imminent danger they were all in, Zara's heart accelerated and she got nervous. Her fear went up her spine and she broke out in a cold sweat, making her forehead wet. Her peer E.T.s exchanged glances finding that unusual.

Even her finger tips pulsed, and the sensations were so many that she couldn't think of all of them at the same time. In a sudden, the woman realized she could not swallow well and felt that something terrible was about to happen. For a moment, Nicholas looked at her and saw how pale she was. Not knowing how he could help her, the young man came up to her and hugged her tight, showing his love for her and trying to calm her down. Feeling better and protected, the doctor once again oversaw the situation, and looked like she was even enjoying the adrenaline that circulated through her body. Little by little, she was returning to her old self.

Nicholas, however, was impressed with the ups and downs of her physical and emotional conditions.

"What happened to you, Zara?"

"Don't worry, Nick. It happens sometimes. In the beginning, I felt scared and panicked, but now I know nothing is going to happen and I even enjoy the temporary energetic sensation it causes. It's just anxiety. I became nervous hearing that Merko was close. Everybody on planet Life know about how efficient he is on every duty of his."

"We, humans, also feel that, even more in stressing situations such as these we're facing now." He spoke. "I thought psychological pathologies, like anxiety and depression, didn't happen in the future."

"The human mind is a good source of knowledge, Nick. Each human being must experience his or her own emotions. Of course, we have many problems in future, and they are the result of our choices and some decisions we must make. On our spaceship, for instance, we have medication for all kinds of pathologies, physical or emotional. However, on the psychological field, the best antidote is to learn to use your own thoughts to deal with personal conflicts and try to solve them."

They both talked peacefully while the others moved away, for them to be more comfortable. The woman took advantage of the moment and opened her heart to tell him all the truth about her mission.

"First, I grew close to you in order to seduce you. I was trained to learn everything about you: what you like, your favorite foods and drinks, what kind of girls you like most. But the more we got close to each other, the more I started having feelings for you that I had never experienced before. Since I'm a doctor, I was chosen to take care of you during your journey to planet Life, so that you arrived in good health to save our Princess."

"But why didn't you tell me the truth?"

"Because I needed to take you with me. If you refused to come, there wouldn't be a chance for Princess Isadora."

"Why didn't you clone me or take some of my marrow?"

"There could be some damage to the material during the return journey and there is no time to risk it."

"Everything had seemed so true, but now... I suspect I was nothing more than part of an assignment." The boy said, heartbroken.

"Oh, please, don't say that, Nick. When I got involved with you, I put everything I believed in aside. Even the survival of our Princess was put in second place. I love you, more than anything else, and I've never thought I'd be able to experience such a thing like that."

"In truth, I don't know if this is right."

"Listen to me, Nick. Before I fell for you, I had a mission to accomplish. I know I should not have used you to meet my goals, but there's a life at stake. The life of a child! If I hurt you, I beg you to forgive me, and I promise I'll make your decision worth every second that's left of our lives."

"Everything you've just said is very beautiful, but I'm upset and, to tell you the truth, I notice myself being used by you, or maybe by your whole team, by your King or whoever. I want to be with you very much, Zara. You are the one I've always dreamed about and, I don't know why, but even after learning the truth about everything, I still feel something so special about you that I'm still able to date you, and maybe let our relationship grow..."

"Let my love add on to yours, Nick. If what we feel for each other can be as big as the Universe, you can be certain that it's just the start in your planet."

He felt a huge desire to kiss her. She realized it and touched his lips with hers. But aware of her peers on the command room next to them, the doctor rationally moved away from Nicholas.

"I want to be with you, Zara. I want to help you save your Princess."

His fear now was just one: to be away from his beautiful and unique beloved. He wanted to help her however he could. On the other hand, he couldn't lose her, not now that he had found her as if finding a star in the vastness of the Cosmos.

He put his right hand on her hand. The woman glanced at Sivoc through the door, saw that he still talked to Tibor and Drako, and slightly pulled her hand away.

"The one thing I ask of you is to come back with me after we save your Princess Isadora, because I can't live away from my family."

"My dear, I have a life in my planet too. I have a job, my father and mother, my siblings. I don't think I could stand living away from them either. Same as you, I'd like to be close to them because I also love them very much."

"You promised me that you'd bring me back after the end of the mission. What I'm asking you now is that, besides bringing me back home, you also be a part of my home."

Zara looked through the glass wall and watched the fish that swam around on the deepest part of the ocean. After some moments of thought, she smiled softly.

"I'll think about all this fondly. Besides that, with the space-ships from the future, I think we'll be able to see my relatives whenever we wish."

"So... Is that a yes?"

She nodded and smiled.

Chapter 11

Meanwhile, in planet Life, counselor Mirov monitored all Sivoc's and counselor Kenan's conversations, and he had a facial expression of pure satisfaction for being able to spy the scientific team's movements.

"Commander Sivoc, the Princess won't last long if she doesn't get the appropriate treatment, and King Zador is under strong emotional pressure because of her. We need to help him. The Board of Counselors hasn't met yet to decide what should be done if the King is proved unable to rule due to his daughter's disease. His love for her is notorious to all."

"We already have the boy with us, Kenan. And we'll depart in a few days. We will keep you informed as soon as we trespass the space-time tunnel."

"Have a nice journey, Captain. I hope you are successful in your mission."

"I have no doubt that, with another loss, the King will be drawn into a deep depressive state, and my chances of ruling will be huge if we accomplish our mission. I will prove myself the most capable of all members of the Board to rule. I already have spies watching the royal family night and day and, just in case it is necessary to take the power by force as an alternative plan, I still have the army on my side. Either way, this planet will be mine! First, I must poison the old nurse who takes care of the girl and, once she dies, I will recommend a substitute nurse that will be under my command. I'll make her change the medications the Princess takes to attenuate the effects of her disease, and maybe she'll die before the expected time. If she does not die and I must bring in the earthling, I'll count on Captain Merko's mission's success to stand out among the members of the Royal Board on a possible election for a new King", thought the diabolic Mirov, exercising all his cruelty.

Mirov, who was in the same room as Radof, exited the communication frequency and contacted Merko. His image soon showed up on a hologram in front of him.

"We've intercepted signs of communication from Sivoc's ship," the counselor said.

"Please, send us the location coordinates, Sir."

"Radof hasn't defined where the signal came from with accuracy yet but, according to him, he'll get them in a few hours. I'll keep you informed."

"Yes, sir! We'll be waiting."

During a meeting, the ship Science's crew concluded that some especial knowledge would be necessary for the terrestrial boy's survival.

"I suggest Nicholas undergoes a microchip implant in his retina so that he can have straight access to information from our database. He'll be permanently linked to our X2 computer."

Tibor, a well-built man, came close to them.

"I'll train him in every fighting technique available. Somebody needs to teach him how to protect himself of all coming hazards. Besides, I'd very much like to do it."

"What do you think about that, Nick?" Zara asked him.

"Will I learn how to read minds as you do?"

"Yes, you will, but it requires a longer training. For now, you'll learn the main fighting techniques and how to unite body and mind into working together. That's why Tibor will teach you."

"With a skinny frame such as that you're gonna have to work out a lot," Tibor laughed. "I'll also bring you some food supplements and special vitamins that I have in stock, suitable to train thin guys."

"Uh... I'm not so sure. Is that a hundred percent safe?"

"My dear, don't worry, I'll take care of you in person. This kind of microchip implant procedure is my area of expertise," the woman told him in order to calm him down.

Nicholas smiled at her. In fact, he was curious to use his new friends' technologies and, most of all, learning to fight would be a privilege.

They started to prepare for the implant. The doctor made use of a tranquilizer gun to shoot the boy's arm with sedatives so that he could relax. Then, she shot him with a painkiller, and he was put on a surgery table. After he underwent a 3D scanner, the computer X2 built his skull prototype, which indicated the best access to his retina for the incision. Taking advantage of the surgery, they also made another insertion - this time in the young man's hippocampus - in order to improve and multiply his memory storage, and another microchip was implanted in his temporal lobe in order to allow future transmutations.

The woman was by the earthling's side during the whole time and watched his recovery. Some hours later, he woke up a bit stunned and, little by little, regained full consciousness. Then, he looked at the lamps on the ceiling, put his hands on the sides of the surgical table and recognized it as the ship Science's surgical room. He fixed his eyes onto the person who gazed at him and realized it was Zara, his love, who was always by his side. He also saw the nurses that had helped with the procedures and the robotic arms on the surgical tables.

"It seems like many things changed in my mind. Everything I see seems to bring me linked information", he thought.

"Nick, are you alright? How do you feel?"

"Yep. I can see you. If I died, I must be in heaven."

She smiled. "Let's go to the recovery room next door. There, we'll wait a while until you're better."

The doctor went along with the young man to the recovery room. There, she pressed a button on the wall and an image of Sivoc showed.

"Captain, any signal of the enemy's ship?"

"Not yet, but we need to get out of here as soon as possible. How is Nicholas doing?"

"He's fine, sir. The surgery was successful".

"Great. Now we can start the procedures of getting out of the spaceship and leaving it in hibernation."

The doctor turned his eyes to the boy and talked about the surgery.

"We implanted some microchips in your body, Nick. One of them will allow you to transmute genetically. You'll be able to transform yourself into one of us when you find it necessary. The other chip will allow you to access information from our database, and a third one increased your memory storage."

"That's why I felt a bit strange when I woke up. I think I am going to like this." The young man said with a slight smile and still feeling relaxed.

The earthling realized in a sudden that he knew the mechanism of all things he saw and touched, and that his mind was processing things at a higher speed than before. At first, he seemed to be out of himself, oblivious to what the others were saying. He stopped, stared at things, and figured out what they were made of and how they functioned. Then, he went back to himself. The young man smiled and felt the power knowledge had granted him. Now it was time for him to go back to his new normal life and brace himself for the difficult days that were on his way.

Sometime later, Zara put her hand on her lover's right hand, took him to the front of the ship and tried to help him.

"Don't you worry about all these changes, Nick. I'll be by your side so that you learn to deal with all these things. More important than knowing how to fight is the knowledge you have now, and that can help you find solutions for many different problems that might come up."

Tibor stood by Nicholas.

"Give me you right arm, boy."

He took off the bracelet and reprogrammed it.

"This is a bracelet from our planet. I don't know how you got it, but it is able to teleport you directly to the ship or anywhere else on planet Earth. A blue light selector indicates the ship and a red-light orients to places selected by the latitude and longitude coordinates you establish. After the first transport, the instrument creates a memory, which will later be selected with a simple touch."

Nicholas looked at that wonderful object on his wrist and his eyes widened with amazement. He didn't know how he got that technological bracelet in the past, but he was very pleased to have it in the present. It was hard for him to hide his excitement.

"Gosh! This is so cool! It's just amazing... I like it very much."

Tibor, Drako and Zara all smiled at the boy's excitement. Now, it was time to leave the spacecraft. Danger was going in their direction and, the more invisible they were, the better. Nick's training was about to start.

Chapter 12

The four members of spaceship Science's crew were still planning on how and where to hide until the day of their return to their planet. A few days had already passed by and Sivoc knew captain Merko would find their ship very soon. Thus, they decided that the safest thing to do would be to leave the spaceship and teleport themselves to New York. Nicholas himself had suggested it, since he had an old dream of visiting that place. That was one of the biggest cities in the world, after all, and it would be very hard to be found among so many people.

They would also start to train the earthling, and to find a place where it could be done with no interruptions was a must-do. The rest of the crew was told to disperse all over the city. They should check in at hotels, get jobs, and be very careful not to be identified by human beings. They wouldn't be there for long and would be informed as soon as Sivoc needed them.

The commander knew all Merko wanted was the boy, and that the captain would never destroy the scientific ship, which was good for them, since they needed the spaceship Science to go back home.

Zara helped the boy set the teleport coordinates on his bracelet, and he waited with anxiety for the departure time.

"We are done."

"I can't believe I'll visit the Big Apple at last! That was always a dream of mine, although I live on the other end of the country."

"Did you say big apple? Are you planning on eating apples over there?" The woman asked.

"No, Zara", he smiled. "That's just a metaphor. The city is called that for historical reasons. In the beginning of the twentieth century, the United States shared its resources among the states as if it were a huge tree, and since New York got a good amount of government money, people started to call it the Big Apple. Moreover, this city was also a strong apple exporter in the seventies, and it started to use this nickname to boost tourism. The marketing ads consisted in showing red apples in order to attract visitors to the city."

"How interesting! I like the culture of your country very much."

Nicholas blushed. It was the moment of departure and he was surprised when his beloved and him teleported and embodied in an alley, behind an old theater on the 46th

Street. He looked at the other three men that, in a sudden, showed up by his side, bearing a sort of calmness proper to those who had done it thousands of occasions before.

"I cannot believe I'm here, alive, after a trip like that with all my cells in their correct place. It sounds crazy!" The young man spoke touching his face to be sure he was there indeed.

"Zara, I want to visit the whole city with you."

"Slow down, Nick. We will have time for that, let's settle ourselves first."

As if he hadn't heard what she had just said, the boy couldn't stop himself and left the alley in a hurry to get to the avenue. The redhead ran right behind him.

"Wait for us, Nick!"

The young man turned his eyes to the sky and saw the skyscrapers. Yellow cabs drove by taking or leaving passengers at the sidewalks, crowded with people who walked as if they were late for a meeting. He looked up at the luminous billboards and colorful banners spread everywhere. They were just where he had thought they would be, and the earthling knew he could go to Madison Square, Central Park, and everything else the Big Apple had to offer.

"You'll have plenty of time to have fun here, Nick, but now we have to go," Tibor said with a stern face when the other three got close.

Drako smiled at the boy's reaction, and Sivoc took them to an apartment in Madison Square Garden, on the 8th Avenue.

The commander asked them all to stay the longest possible in the hotel.

In the meantime, the specialist in information accessed the Terrestrial Identification Systems, and all of them were given new IDs. They had exchanged their planet's gold for American money and asked X2 to prepare some credit cards for them with enough to support them during their stay in New York. Everything was done as requested, and he saw the credit cards materialize on his apartment table. It was also easy for him to get into the Information Systems and find some temporary jobs for each one of them. Besides, he would also choose jobs they would fit better in, and they would live comfortably in the city.

* * *

On a Friday night, Zara and Nicholas went to the movies. The full moon in the sky created an atmosphere that made the couple even more intimate than they already were. The woman's beauty was the one thing the boy had eyes for, which had attracted him since the very first moment, and he did his best not to think that it could change some day. Both were taking a walk in Central Park when she grabbed his hand.

"Nick, I'm not sure if we should get this involved with each other."

"Zara, please, there is nothing more important to me than being with you, here or anywhere else."

She answered his loving eyes, and they decided to watch a love story, since she had never felt those feelings the way human beings do here on Earth. Everything was too different in planet Life, too planned and artificial when compared to the things she was experiencing with her love on Earth.

"Life is so good here on Earth. Couples kiss and hug in such a romantic aura. Happy parents and children play in the parks. What a wonderful thing to see... I think it's wonderful. On Life, people almost don't go out for entertainment; they are so addicted to technology, that they also use it on a large scale to have fun. And people's love for each other slips through their fingers along with their own lives," the E.T. thought.

As soon as the movie ended, they went back to the apartment and everything was silent again. Looking into Nicholas' eyes, the woman remembered their time together at the shack, and her desire to be with him increased. She was worried about the commander's reaction, but her desire was stronger than that.

Meanwhile, the young man prepared a dish with several types of cheese, and took it to her room. To drink, he opened a bottle of wine and poured it for his beloved one. Before starting to eat, though, he caressed her red hair and touched his lips on hers, feeling her warm body.

"You, humans, like to taste many flavors at the same moment..." She commented in a playful way.

"Despite the fabulous flavor of this wine, I still prefer the flavor of the honey I taste on your lips", Nicholas said. "I've never thought I'd go out with a physician. Especially a beautiful, clever, tender one and, most important of all, from another planet."

"And I find you magnificent, Nick. I've never had the things I have achieved by your side: kindness, sweet words and generosity. I love you."

The young man kissed her mouth, and the woman let her emotions set free. Her heart beat frantically, but it wasn't because of stress now. It was because of the pleasure of being with someone she loved... They smiled at each other, and spent one of the happiest nights of their lives together.

"I love you", she whispered in his ear.

"I want to spend the rest of my live with you. I love you too, Zara."

He, who had already imagined that moment many times, knew he should overcome his shyness in order to be with her. Then, the two of them decided to let themselves be guided by love and were lost in the caresses of each other. Nicholas touched the pale skin of his beloved's shoulders in a soft way, kissed her neck and put aside a strand of her soft hair from the redhead's blue eyes.

Then, he put down the strap of her shirt and waited for her to take her clothes off. His eyes lingered on her, admiring her shape as if she were a piece of art. Few times in his life, he had been so happy and excited.

With a tight hug, as if entering inside her depths, he surrendered to love. They both gave themselves into that endless moment, getting familiar to feelings they had never imagined before. Afterwards, exhausted but pleased, they fell asleep for some minutes to wake up in the arms of each other. So, they cuddled, just enjoying each other's company.

"This was the best day of my entire life", Nicholas said staring at her.

"I've never lived such an intense moment like that either", Zara replied, looking back at him.

Nicholas kissed her.

They loved each other with no eyes for space or time, and then the redhead lied her head on the earthling's arm and they fell asleep for the night.

Meanwhile, the three E.T.s wandered around the city streets. Many bars were open at night, and they decided to go into one of them. A neon sign showed the place's name: Night Drink Bar.

Sivoc wore jeans and a brown leather jacket, Tibor and Drako wore black leather jackets and, when they went into the bar, all clients looked at them: three tall and handsome men with a perfect frame. It didn't take long and three beautiful women got close and shared the table with them.

"Can we keep you company?" One of them asked.

"Make yourself at home", Drako answered with a smile.

"Where are you from, guys?" The friendliest one asked. "I'm Sonja. Nice to meet you. The blonde one here is Alyson, and the brunette is Jessie."

"We are from a very far place, and we're here to visit the city", the commander answered shyly.

"I see. We can show you nice places to go, if you want. You can bet the best things in the world are here in New York."

"I'm sure everything will be very pleasant in the company of such beautiful women like you", the I.T. expert said, being friendly too.

Although a bit embarrassed, the captain enjoyed the place as well as Tibor, who had fun listening to the music played by a band, at the same time he looked at the perfect lips of the blonde next to him.

Tibor served himself with a double shot of whisky and had it at once. The tech guru followed him and commented telepathically with all:

"What a nice shot, uh? I'm going to order another one."

"Take it easy, guys. We can't get distracted. Merko can get here anytime and we have to be prepared for him. Moreover, we're in a mission, don't forget it", Sivoc answered telepathically too.

The three men from Planet Life had a lot of fun that night. Tibor and Drako spent the night with the women. The music was pleasant and they decided to enjoy that night in the bar.

While the two of them had fun and relaxed, very impressed by the way humans from that time knew how to have fun, the commander enjoyed the place too, although keeping his mind alert and thinking of his wife, who was waiting for him on Life. Since he knew it would be hard for Merko to find them, he felt safe for a while.

"How I miss Laiza. I wish she was here now", he thought, while observing the environment. No matter how far he was from home, not just his mind, but also his body were connected to his family. Besides that, his sense of loyalty would never allow him any misbehavior.

* * *

In the alien ship in Alaska, Sanches woke up and tried to figure out where he was.

"Am I dreaming? How did I get here?"

He remembered he had seen an E.T. before fainting, and froze in fear. In a sudden, a door opened in the middle of the wall and a man who resembled a Latin guy approached him. He was tall and strong with broad shoulders.

"Hi, pal. How you feeling? Better?"

"Where am I? And who are you, hombre?"

"Nice to meet you. I'm Merko and you are on a military base."

"But this place is surrounded by a kind of technology I've never seen before", Sanches stated, looking at the holograms that monitored Earth and Life. "And what about those hombres extraños who embodied out of nowhere in my house? What was that?"

"You are right. We're not humans like you are. We are from another planet and we need your help..." Merko went straight to the point.

Sanches almost freaked out again, but he got a grip on himself and balanced himself on his long legs. Although he didn't believe in what was being said, he remembered the E.T. he had seen before he had fainted.

If those guys were genuine E.T.s, what did they want from him? What could he do that was so important? Would they set him free later or would they make him forget everything with a light stick, as they usually did in Sci-Fi movies?

Chapter 13

Merko read Sanches' mind and knew he didn't believe he was among extraterrestrials, although he was astonished with those unexpected guys at his door, with the way they had teleported and with all the technology before him. The vision of the commander in his alien form before he had fainted was still tucked in his throat, even though he still thought it had been a dream or a nervous breakdown.

"This hombre tells me he is an E.T. He must be crazy! I think they have kidnapped me and will ask my mother for ransom. Poor mother! We're not rich, and hers and my father's salaries barely pay my university", the earthling worried.

"Take it easy, Earth boy!" the captain said in advance. "We are not kidnappers and we don't want your family's money either. I'll prove to you we're not from here, but keep calm, please. Do you remember when you were a child and your mom forced you to go to church? Priest Francisco's sermons lasted hours, and you used to be very mad because you had to go with her instead of being home watching TV shows? She also didn't understand that at school, when your friends started to talk about their favorite shows and you had nothing to say, it was a frustration for you …" The young man's eyes got wide with amazement. How could he know about all those things? "Do you need me to tell you more? How about if I talk about Lindy, that girl you were fallen for at school? Do you remember her dark curly hair?"

The earthling was speechless, but he couldn't stop thinki ng… Which meant that nothing had changed for the captain.

"It seems he has read my mind! That's impossible! How can he know the priest's and my childhood crush's names? He must be a mutant that reads thoughts, like those guys from the movies, or maybe a government robot…"

Annoyed with the boy's persisting disbelief, he placed two fingers on his bracelet. There it was… He was an alien again, that figure all human beings were afraid of.

"It must be a dream. This isn't possible! It must be a hallucination. Did you give me anything to drink? Did you put anything in it?"

"Sanches, pay attention!" Merko said out loud. "Look at that transparent wall."

A wall rose at one side of the room where they were in, and the young man saw they were placed on a peak that was very similar to a mountain. He ran to the glass wall, looked down and realized they were over six thousand feet up.

He pondered about saying something, but nothing came out of his mouth. He believed himself delirious. The commander came by and put his left hand over his shoulder to calm him down. Sanches screamed in panic.

Right then, Crom also came up in his extraterrestrial form and made him even more scared.

"How is our visitor doing, Commander?"

"He's doing all right! Still a bit skeptical, though. But I'm sure that he will understand very soon that our eyes never deceive us and that, even if we try to run away from things, we wish weren't real, we have to face the truth someday."

"From what I can see, he's not doing well at all. He's very frightened."

"If all of this is real, what do you expect of me?" Sanches said and moved away from those two creatures. "And why haven't you killed me? Please, kill me but don't do my parents any harm. Where are they? Are you invading my planet?" he blabbed.

"Don't worry, boy," Merko tried to calm him down. "Your family is well and we don't intend to invade your planet. To be honest, we wouldn't have brought you here if you hadn't seen my men teleporting. But, since you watched them, we had to bring you with us and now we need your help."

"But how can I help you? I don't think you need a student who speaks Spanish. I saw your men speaking Spanish in the US."

"I'm not going to hang around with some E.T.s and help them invade Earth," the young man thought again, unaware that the captain could read his mind.

"Take it easy. It has nothing to do with that. I'm just looking for a friend of yours."

"Ok, don't tell me... It's about Nicholas again. That's what they asked me at home... And I 've told them everything I know."

"Sure. But there's one piece of information missing: what's the name of the girl you met and where is she from?"

"I won't tell you anything else."

"What the hell is going on with Nick? Why do those aliens want to put their hands on him so much?"

The captain felt there was something wrong in the way Sanches referred to Nicholas, and could vision the argument he and his friend had had as soon as he was told Nick and Zara were going out together.

"Why are you so protective of your friend? He went out with the hottest girl of school, the one all of you had a crush on, and he told you nothing about it! It seems he doesn't trust you at all. So, why protect him so much? Besides, we won't do you any harm. Zara... Is that her name?" Merko asked.

"You're right... It's Zara. But how did you hear about that?"

"Someone told us at the university."

Still mad at Nicholas, the boy told him everything.

"Zara, the most beautiful chica of all, showed up at the university and Nicholas fell in love with her right away. They couldn't take their eyes off each other and I encouraged him to get close to her."

"I see… That makes me want to learn everything I can about your friend. Do you have any idea where he could be now?"

"I have no idea of what else to say. Oh God! Nick hasn't said a word about his date with the chica. I don't even know if we are such close friends anymore. But I'll tell this man everything I remember. I won't make up anything. If I do so, maybe they'll leave me alone and decide not to attack my family", the earthling thought.

"He was going out with the chica, but, even though I'm a close friend of his, I was the last one to have knowledge about it."

Merko and Crom looked at each other, and the captain raised an eyebrow being surprised with Sanches' reaction.

"Crom, let's go back to our terrestrial form. He's cooperating and telling us everything he knows, even things that we aren't interested in", the commander said telepathically.

They went back to their human forms to make him more comfortable.

"You look much better this way," the earthling affirmed.

The captain smiled at Crom as he fingered through the grey tufted hair that hung on his forehead.

"Let's release him. I think he has already told us everything he knows about his friend. I'm almost sure Sivoc's team has hidden the spaceship somewhere on Earth. They must be mixed among human beings. We shall find Science ship. Then, we hack their computer and find some clues of their whereabouts."

"Thank you, lad. You were of great value for us", he thanked him.

But the young man was filled with remorse. He regretted saying anything.

"I shouldn't have told them anything at all. Nick was always a nice guy, and he may be in danger. I wonder what these men want from him ¡Que Dios nos proteja!"

"Take the boy to the nursery and delete his memory up to the point when he saw our men at his house. He won't remember a single thing and he'll feel better. Then, teleport him back to his home." Captain Crom ordered telepathically.

Sanches observed another two men coming out of a door on the wall. Along with Crom, they escorted him to the infirmary. There was no way to fight back.

On their way, the earthling observed the hallways. They were lit by a blue light that drew a central line on the floor and a continuous strip of lamps on both sides of the ceilings. Then, a door opened and he could see the medical room. There, he also saw a nurse wearing a mask and a white uniform as well as a man with a silver uniform that made him look like a doctor. Before he could say anything, somebody came from behind him and shot him on the neck. He fell asleep.

A while later, he was in his garage, minutes before his mother found him fainted on the floor.

"Mi querido hijo! Usted está allí. Por favor, despierta!"

The young man opened his eyelids.

"What happened, mamá?" He asked, unaware of what had happened to him.

"I don't know, my dearest. I thought you knew what had happened and would be able to tell me. ¿Are you well?"

"¡Si, mamá!"

"Lo que importa es que tú estás bien, mi querido hijo."

The boy had a headache and closed his eyes pressing onto them hoping the pain would cease. When he did that, though, he visualized an E.T. Afraid of what he had seen, he looked up to the sky in order to check if he would see anything.

"What the hell was that?" He wondered.

The image, in fact was nothing more than an after effect of what he had lived. Sanches believed he had had a bad dream and that image might have been the last thing he had lived in his nightmare.

In the quietness of his bedroom, he had many similar dreams during the following months.

* * *

Meanwhile, Merko planned talking to Crom his next step in order to be successful in his mission.

"We must locate the Scientific spaceship, find the boy and take him with me to planet Life. We have to save Princess Isadora. Zara used her female gifts in the shape of a beautiful woman to seduce the young man and take him with her. As for Sivoc, I know him as well as all his team, and I'm sure they are all honorable people. I can't understand why they're hiding from me since we could work together. Maybe they want to take over the mission and gain prestige with the government. Two task forces were chosen in order to avoid failures in the mission. If one of them were caught by Earth's governments, the other would go on and nothing would be lost. That's why we were chosen to save the mission. Everyone knows I've never failed before and I won't miss the opportunity to save our next Queen's life now, at any costs."

Chapter 14

Drako teleported to Science ship at the bottom of the sea and picked up an amphibious transport ship. It would be a strategic means of transport if anything happened to the scientific spacecraft. Drako rented a warehouse on the outskirts of the city where he kept the ship in safety.

The other day, Sanches was getting ready to take the bus to college when two motorcycles stopped in front of him. The pilot of one of them raised his helmet. It was Drako. Behind him another man raised his visor, Tibor.

Sanches once again almost fainted thinking it was a robbery. However, a familiar voice called to him on the motorcycle right behind them.

"Friend, get on my motorcycle here."

His eyes widened.

"Nick! Where were you and who are these guys? The police are looking for you."

"There's no time, Sanches! I'll tell you everything when we're safe. Get up here quick!"

"All right, hermano."

They accelerated as the bike began to transform into an aerial vehicle resembling a drone. Suddenly, they were flying...

"Hombre, are you sure you know how to drive this thing? It can't be you. I've never imagined you riding a motorcycle."

"Rest assured! I'm learning things you would never believe."

With Sanches scared, they continued their journey through the skies until they teleported to a warehouse in New York.

When they got there, the Latino watched everything, looked at Zara and she greeted him, and he saw the alien ship in a corner.

"Wow, hombre! How much technology... And Zara? Is the college babe with you? And the motorcycle that flies? I'll have one of these for myself when I work. What about these guys? That ship? Is this a movie set? And why did you disappear? Your mother is crazy looking for you."

"Calm down, friend! I promised you I would explain everything. Zara asked me a favor. And I needed to be gone for a while."

"What?"

"It's just... it's... My friends here are from another planet."

"Ha, ha, ha... Can you tell me another joke? That was awesome. What about Zara?"

"She's also an alien."

'That's what I thought."

"So do you believe me?"

"No, I think you are crazy. Studying too much can make one go mad, see? But I can help you. My mother knows a psychiatrist who is very good."

"You are mistaken, Sanches." He spoke.

"Let me help you, Nick."

Zara interceded to help. She touched her bracelet and began to writhe in pain. Suddenly, she had changed.

The young man looked at the others and they were also in extraterrestrial form to show the truth so difficult to explain. She telepathically asked them for assistance.

Sanches looked like he was going to freak out. Nicholas took his arm and supported him.

"It was better to show you the reality that no words of mine could tell."

The Latin stopped, looked at everything carefully and said:

"Hombre, in college I thought you finally got along with a woman and were going to date. But now I see you're in trouble. And why did you bring me here? This is the last place I wanted to be."

"We're going to travel to another planet and save a girl and maybe the entire population. I think you will enjoy exploring other worlds."

"If I have a choice, I want to go home."

"Come on, Sanches. In no cosmology class will you learn as much as on this trip."

"Ok! I will, but I need to tell my mother. She's going to freak out and look like Lorena."

"I think you'd better not."

"Why?"

"There are some guys from Planet Life after us. When we get back, Zara and his friends have promised to return us by this date and no one will miss us."

"Just what I needed. Now there will be time travel too."

"We'll explain everything during the trip, Sanches." Zara said after returning to her human form.

"Madre mia... I hope I'm making the right decision."

Nicholas told the whole story to his friend and, observed by him, trained all modalities of fighting. Although he had the theories in his mind, he needed his figure to be well built and in good health to harmonize his training in order to control his inner energy.

After the first exercises, in a few days, he started showing great results and had the ability to perform all his master's lessons.

After a lot of practice, the alien instructor invited him to train on improvised tatami in the warehouse. Unable to resist such an invitation, he accepted to fight. It was about time to check his learning. Sanches and the other watched their battle.

The trainer nailed some punches, but the boy noticed that he knew the right vulnerable spots on the opponent's body, and aimed at them. His teacher, on the contrary, was an expert at fighting with both legs and arms, whether he was attacking or defending. The combat was hard to win, and the young man tried to find a way to knock his adversary out. In a blink of an eye, he grabbed his professor by the arms, picked up steam, wedged onto his rival's feet and dropped him on the floor. Then he jumped on him in order to pin him down to perform an armlock and, so, end his stunt.

At that moment, his adversary hit his leg three times, giving up on the round. So, the earthling apologized and offered his hand to help him get up.

"Very nice, Nicholas. You are a fast learner and you're using your right hand as well as the armlock pretty well... That's very good!" The master said, admired.

The young man thanked him, his body aching. Tibor was much bigger than him.

On the second round of the training, the teacher decided to take him to a deserted place so that they could train in different scenarios, using the best weapons they had. From that day on, the two of them teleported themselves to a deserted spot in the Grand Canyon, Arizona. Besides training at the school, they went to the desert every day. Sanches accompanied them and learned to throw some punches.

The trainer taught the boy how to use the weapons. There was a spear, made of a kind of stick which unfolded, projecting laser rays out of its two sides. He also had a laser pistol and a sound wave ring that was perfect for making the opponents lose their balance. A cosmic ray launcher pierced big holes on its targets. All of them were very powerful guns.

Tibor's teaching essence was to show the earthling that, above all, the most important thing to learn in the art of combat was honor, character, and altruism.

After watching Nicholas at the end of an exhaustive day of training, the mentor told him:

"You are almost ready, lad. Throughout this week, I could see your physical and mental improvement. You're stronger today and you're not that skinny guy I met before. Congratulations, my friend!"

In no time, the young man would know that everything he had learnt would be very precious and useful for a real fight.

As soon as he had a break, Nicholas went out for a ride with his love. Sanches stayed with Drako and Tibor listening to the stories of his space adventures. The couple enjoyed the Saturday afternoon off and left to the Central Park. That day, there were many famous actors acting out in an outdoor performance. New Yorkers and tourists used to wait for hours in line for the show and, while they walked hand to hand, the boy saw the long line and suggested:

"How about we watch the play, Zara? It was written by a famous writer from the XVI century, William Shakespeare."

"I loved the idea", the woman said.

"However, we'll have to wait on this very long line. I heard people saying they've been waiting here since earlier today."

"That is okay. I'm having a lot of fun here with you. I'm going to tell Sivoc that we'll get to the hotel a bit later tonight."

The redhead contacted the commander so that he wouldn't be worried about them, and explained they would watch a show that was being performed at the park. Sivoc asked them to be careful and avoid any kind of trouble there.

The young couple stayed in line along with other folks who were anxious for the play that would be performed in an open theater in the middle of the park, as it happened traditionally. The earthling bought ice-cream for both, and they were enjoying the moment very much.

"Have you ever heard of William Shakespeare?" He asked her.

"I've heard something about him in my Earth Culture classes. If I'm not mistaken, he was a great writer."

"He was one of the greatest writers of all times. He was born in England, wrote poetry, plays and many texts that are considered masterpieces up to today. The piece we're about to watch is one of his most famous ones and I'm sure you'll love it. It's called Hamlet, and it's staged all over the world. It's about a prince from Denmark who wants to get back at his uncle Claudio, who has killed his father. Despite not being a murderer, Hamlet experiences the dilemma to fulfill or not his revenge plan. There's one important sentence that you'll hear on the performance, and that's "To be or not to be, that's the question", and the author often says it while holding a skull."

"Wow, Nick, I had already heard something about the author, but you gave me such an excellent explanation about it! Now, I'll get the most out of the show when we watch it. When you told me about Hamlet, I imagined myself with a skull in my hands, thinking of how much I love you and how much I want to live with you in your planet. And asking myself: 'To be or not to be an E.T.? That's the question!'"

They both broke into a laugh and weren't able to stop laughing until the play was on the stage. After the show, they went for another stroll.

"We must go back now, dear. We've been out for a while", Zara said.

Hours passed by and, when they realized it was night already, three guys moved toward them suddenly, in a very suspicious way, and one of them shouted in a rude voice:

"Two lovebirds lost in the park, what a nice couple you are! Give me all your money, now!"

"Don't worry, Zara," Nicholas whispered. "Keep calm."

"I said now! Did you get it? We're not kidding, dude. Now!" The other guy demanded, pointing a gun at them.

The woman held onto her lover firmly and broke out in a cold sweat. Her forehead was wet and her fingers pulsed. Her heart was accelerated and she couldn't swallow well. Nick saw how pale she was, got frightened and looked at the bad guys. Then, he stared at the man in front of him with such an intense anger that his gun started to levitate. The same happened with the other guys' guns, which were released from their hold and thrown over ten yards away. Then, the three men started to levitate too. The boy stared at them and made them go up in the air, panicking and yelling for help. They were then released at the top of a tree close to the bridge where they had been.

"Zara, what are you doing? Stop it... Otherwise you're going to kill these men", the young man asked.

The three men hung like fruit from a tree, while Zara recovered little by little. Nicholas looked at her, disturbed.

"What was that about? I'm so amazed! How could you lift those men as if they were mere feathers, and place them so high in the trees?"

"It wasn't me, love. I'd never do such a thing. I think it was you who did it," she stated, in amazement. "We should run now. We must get out of here. There's a subway station near here with few people around at this time of the night. We can hide there for a while and teleport to the hotel."

They went to the station and then straight to their apartment. The woman was very impressed with what she had just seen, since almost no one in her world had developed the ability called telekinesis. There was one person she knew that could do it: Merko. Even though almost everybody knows how it works, this was a very special ability limited to very few humans. There was a rumor going around planet Life that Merko could move objects and throw them at their opponents. Some also said that he could also channel cosmic radiations, launch powerful rays with his very own hands and make the enemy decay. Besides that, the citizens mentioned he had the ability to control the force of gravity. He had become a legend in his planet.

"How could Nick use telekinesis with those thieves? I wonder if he has any extraterrestrial genetic heritage," the E.T. thought, amazed with her beloved's mind skill. "And that bracelet he says he won. Whose was it?"

Surrounded by the warm atmosphere of the apartment, the earthling continued talking about how they had gotten rid of the three thieves:

"You said you believe that it was me who did that. How could I? What sort of power is that?"

"It's telekinesis, the ability to dominate gravitational forces."

"Zara, you may have that talent, but might just be able to use it when you are under strong emotional tension and anger."

"No, Nick. It was not me; it was you! Somehow you can move things. I know one person on my planet that knows how to do that, and that's one of the reasons everybody fears him. We'll have to learn more about it later. To me, it would be hard to believe it if I had not seen it with my very own eyes. And you're going to have to control it with mastery, for it is dangerous."

"Who has that power?"

"Merko, the man who is looking for you. Do you understand now why we're so worried about him and the consequences of his actions for all of us?"

Nicholas nodded. He was afraid of his own gift. He couldn't understand how he had developed it and, most of all, how he would learn to use it well. He yawned and looked at his love.

"I'm tired, dear."

"I know, we need to get some rest. You, most importantly. Telekinesis requires lots of energy, especially from a person like you, with almost no training."

The boy went to bed and tried to sleep.

"Nick seems to be more complex than I could ever imagine. Lymphocytes N, telekinesis... I wonder if he has an alien DNA. Or is there another explanation for that?" The woman thought, looking at him.

Chapter 15

Nicholas was tired and couldn't understand how those things had happened to him. He could not believe he had had the power to lift those thieves some feet above the ground, as well as to take their guns out of their hands. Lying in bed, he spent some time looking at the ceiling thinking of his mom and his little sister. He remembered the way his sister used to go to his bedroom and ask him to tell her some stories, and he missed her so much that his eyes were soon filled with tears.

"How can I be away from them? How long will it take for me to go back home? Oh, how I miss my family. I wish I could be in touch with them to explain that I'm fine, but I also know it would make them vulnerable to danger. Sivoc's right, it's better to leave them unaware of my whereabouts. I just hope they aren't suffering too much with my absence."

Thoughts like those, about the people he was forced to leave, devastated him, until the moment he was overcome by sleep.

* * *

Zara got into her lover's room and spent some minutes looking at him, who was in deep sleep. She thought about everything that happened at the park, and decided to inform her friends who were resting in the living room. The captain, Drako and Tibor listened to her.

"I'm sure it's an incredible ability of his, and I don't believe the microchips we implanted are the source of that power."

"If not, what's the explanation?" Sivoc asked. "Drako, being a specialist in Information Systems, could you tell us?"

"I know nothing at all about telekinesis. As well as everyone on our planet, I have just heard many stories about Merko's gift. But I've never seen it happen, and to me it was nothing but a myth."

They looked at Sanches and Zara asked the boy:

"Have you ever seen anything like this when you were around your friend?"

"Never!" He was also puzzled.

"Anyway, even not being aware of the source of his skill, we must train him. I'll help him channel his talent and use it the best way possible, without any waste of stamina."

All of them agreed with Tibor, and Zara relaxed because, if Nick used his power with wisdom, he could protect himself better. As soon as Nicholas woke up, she would explain him about his new training.

Meanwhile, the earthling had a terrible dream. His family was in danger. Many dangerous E.T.s had broken into his house, and one of them was going straight to Sophia's bedroom, while another one went to his mother's. He broke out in a cold sweat... Things started to move in a frenetic way in their rooms and furniture and other objects were being thrown through the window. Suddenly, in his dream, a very strong force field put the E.T.s in a jail made of energy, and he himself, despite being asleep, was nervous, shaking his head from side to side.

In his bedroom, at the hotel, the boy was frightened. The feeling of power blew up inside him, and all the objects around started moving too. The lamp was thrown against the wall and the two nightstands broke apart.

With all that noise, Zara got into his room breathless and saw the light flashing on and off.

"Nick, wake up! Wake up!" She yelled shaking his wet head. Nicholas woke up and sat up in astonishment.

Everyone woke up worried and Sanches was even more nervous about all that mystery.

* * *

At the North of the planet, Merko widened his eyes; he was at the base and noticed an abnormal activity in the air, an impressive peak of energy.

"What is that?! It seems someone is using the power of telekinesis here on Earth. That's impossible! Nobody has that gift here!"

* * *

The earthling opened his eyes and realized that those things were nothing but a bad dream. The woman helped him recover from the nightmare with a glass of water and a bit of love. She told him that, from then on, he would have to learn to use his skill with wisdom. The place was a complete mess.

"Did I do this? But how come...?"

"Your new ability must be controlled, love. It seems you had a bad dream, and look at what happened."

Drako and Sivoc got into the room to see what had taken place there. Sanches came right behind them looking at the mess with wide eyes.

"It seems everything you told us about the boy is too little compared to reality, Zara", Sivoc said.

"There's one thing I know for sure: when he gets to our planet, I won't let him spend one single night at my house," Drako said in a smile.

"This is not a joke, Drako, we have a situation here! Tibor needs to help the boy control his ability as soon as possible. If used with wisdom, it'll be of great advantage to us."

"You can move everything you want with the power of your thoughts, Nick."

"But this has never happened before. What have you done to me? Was it an effect of the surgery?" The young man wanted to know.

"No. No way. Such a gift is for very few people. We'll find out how you developed it. The most important thing now is to learn how to deal with it, and use it to your advantage", the woman answered.

The chief of security took him to the desert, to the same place where they had been going every day to train with weapons and laser rays, and started training him that very same day. Once there, the trainer asked him to move a huge stone that was placed on the top of a mountain.

"Nicholas, you can make use of the cosmic energies released by the stars and channel them into your body. Just focus on that strength and have faith in your skill. Then, make sure that power flows through you and guide it to your hands. It will be released through your fingers to the object you want to move. Or destroy."

The earthling did as he had been told. He focused on the stone and tried to absorb the cosmic energy. Although he was shivering on the inside and felt his blood spread all over his being, nothing different happened.

"I just can't do it again. It was not me."

"Just focus, Nick, and believe in yourself. If you try hard, you'll get it", Tibor said.

The young man just couldn't do it anymore and, skeptical as he was about the source of that gift, he wanted to give up. But his trainer insisted that that was not a possibility, and that "believing" was the primary requirement for any mental power. He insisted so much that Nicholas ended up having an outburst:

"It's no use to stand here trying over and over again! You all push very hard on me while you have in fact changed my entire world and I don't even know if all of this is something I want to do for sure. All I want is to have my life back! One more thing: you're all crazy to think I can move objects!"

"Listen to me, lad: I heard you were a skinny pale guy that your colleagues at college used to laugh at and call Moon boy. Is that old status something you want for yourself? Even with the hard training we've been going through and with you being stronger than you were before, I think that you are still listening to those mocking words. Now, look up at that stone and just move it!" The E.T. ordered in a command voice, making good use of the strength that he knew would be released from the young man's anger.

As the trainer had foreseen, driven by a strong feeling of anger, the earthling looked over at the nine-foot diameter stone and felt a strong energy flow through his body. Then, following the movement of his left hand, the stone started lifting as if it were made of Styrofoam. With his right hand,

Nicholas released a blue Cosmic ray and disintegrated the stone in multiple particles.

"Wow! Didn't I say you could do that? And after some training you'll be able to improve it, and it will be a natural part of your being that will help you protect yourself from incoming danger."

Then the grudge he held for his trainer became amazement, and the boy felt stronger. He then realized that something unique had happened in his existence indeed, and he would have to learn to live with his new powers.

* * *

Life in the capital of the world was still calm, but the spaceship Science team needed to be very discrete as to not reveal their whereabouts. Sivoc put all members of his crew together in the spaceship, the earthling included, since he was now considered a part of his squad. The confrontation between them and Merko's men was approaching, and they'd have to plan some strategies to be followed. They would either have to beat them or hide away.

"What happened, Commander?" The chief of security asked.

"I received a message from our planet saying that Merko already knows about our position. I believe there won't be any other way to deal with them other than a confrontation."

"I'm sure we can fight them, Commander. I'm training the earthling to protect himself, and each of us here already knows how to fight well", Tibor said.

"I still think that running away is the best option, since fighting could be dangerous and we could all die. We also have to protect Nick. We might be able to hide and buy us enough time until the day of our return," Zara commented.

"I'll try to find everything I can about Merko's spaceship's location", Drako interrupted. "Things seem to be more difficult for us. Counselor Kenan told us that he believes there's a traitor among them, for someone intercepted our communication with Life."

"I think the best thing to do now is to teleport to Science ship, where we have some communication and tracking equipment. We also have to make contact with Kenan once more, and that's just possible from the ship."

"Nicholas, this is the opportunity for you to change your form for the first time. You have to get adapted to the different human shape you'll use on our planet. You'll have to look like all of us while you are there", the woman told him.

All of them touched their bracelets and went back to the ship. The earthling then transmuted for the first time and could see himself as one of them. He didn't know why, but he felt very comfortable with his new friends.

Zara took Sanches' hand and led him to the ship as well to keep him close to them.

Nicholas looked at the glass window that reflected his image and realized that his big eyes had a broader lateral field of vision. His skull was bigger too, and it seemed out of proportion compared to the rest of the body. He raised his hand and saw his three fingers. He stretched his tongue to see that it was smaller than it used to be due to his smaller mouth cavity. Now that it was him who had transformed himself, he wondered if he could go back to his original form. He put his fingers on his nostrils and found nothing but two small holes. He breathed harder than usual because breathing seemed to be more difficult with those shrunk nasal cavities but, after some minutes, he got used to them and to his distinct way of breathing. His body ached, since all his molecular structure had changed.

"Where are my ears? And what will I do if everyone vanishes and leaves me alone looking like this? What will I do with my life?" The boy wondered.

"Nick, after some transmutations you'll get used to all the reactions you feel. Sure, it won't be a mild transformation, but I'll be by your side", Zara said, getting close to him and feeling his discomfort.

"Hey, Sanches? Do you believe everything I told you?"

"Of course, I do! I just hope I don't have to change. I prefer to be the way I am."

Nicholas smiled.

Now, they were all in Science ship to try to make contact with the team's planet and get more information about captain Merko, who was at their heels.

Some weeks after his transformation, the earthling hadn't seen himself much in his new shape other than in the image reflected on the glass window. He was both fascinated and surprised. Never in his entire existence could he think he would live so many different situations at the same time. Finding out about living beings on other places in the Universe, all their technologies, as well as explanations about the future of mankind; all this information was fascinating and seemed not to have an end. He was sure that, when he got to Life, he would still find out many more things that he couldn't even imagine. Moreover, seeing his lover as an equal increased even more their mutual kinship.

"Why are you looking at me, Nicholas?"

"Now that I see myself in my extraterrestrial form, the same way I see you, I realize that the love I feel for you goes beyond your figure. It's such an intense feeling that it makes me see deeper inside you and makes me understand how all species in the whole Universe are able to find a match. Even if our young shapes don't change now, one day we'll grow old together, and seeing each other's inside is the most perfect way to find an endless form of love."

"Oh, I love you, sweetheart! You are so handsome!"

While Drako tried to communicate with planet Life, Zara and Nicholas kissed in her room.

That wasn't an appropriate moment for love, though, and they couldn't stick around much longer. At that very moment, they were the prey.